MW01173193

This book is
the Magical property of

_____

First and fully,
to me magical better half,
Madonna Lynn McAllister Uhrain Wyatt,
the most beautiful and amazing creation
the Lord has blessed me to share
me time in this world with.
I love you, Lynnie.

To those who had to become adults when
they were still supposed to be children.
Those who struggle with PTSD,
a battle with one's own mind.
Victims of abuse.
And all those who had their innocence and
childhoods taken due to no part of their own.
The Cancers of the World
Victims to become guardians.
Give it to the King of Kings.

And last, to all me friends and
those who truly understand what
it is to lose loved ones—
To baby Aaron whom I look forward
to walking hand in hand with.
The hole you learn to live with,
never to be filled, only danced around.

To Banish a Tree

PALMETTO
PUBLISHING
Charleston, SC
www.PalmettoPublishing.com

Hardcover ISBN: 979-8-8229-2490-1
Paperback ISBN: 979-8-8229-2491-8
eBook ISBN: 979-8-8229-2492-5

To Banish a Tree

Trickery of a Magical Goat

RJ WYATT

Contents

PREFACE

THIS STORY IS ABOUT A MAGICAL UNDERGROUND world, the World Under, where humans live much as they do above ground. Paul, a wizard, innocent and wrongfully cursed, must spend the rest of his life as a large goat. He has dedicated his life to the service of the royal family's children, watching and protecting them as they live and grow up. He also plays a large part in fighting an evil shadow, a lost soul from the past, as well as the evil that lives in most people's hearts. He takes on a new role as a mentor, going out of his way to help and educate all willing to band together to help in his cause: the recognition of the royal twins, Miranda and Aaron, and their journey to retake a lost world. You will get to enjoy his work and see it become a light to the world we all live in. I hope you all enjoy this creation of a world where magic is as deep as one's ability to imagine, at the same time learning what is most cherished in life: love and relationships.

This story came about because of the loss of friends and family dear to my heart. It has been a tool in coping with these losses and the loss of my childhood. I am loved by me magical soul mate, Lynn. I hope you enjoy me world.

Yours truly,
RJ Wyatt, a follower of Jesus Christ

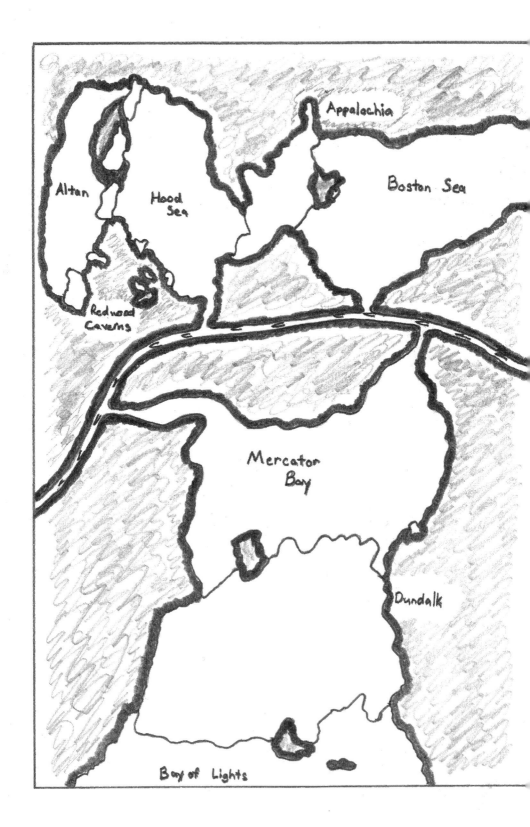

Scottish
Irish Caverns

Sagano
Caverns

Sea of Nessie

Daintree
Sea

Domhan faoi
Thalamh
(World Under)

Queensland

Bay of Lights

THE GUIDE FOR NEW CITIZENS AND MAGICAL TRAVELERS IN THE WORLD UNDER

A Brief Introduction

WELCOME TO, DOMHAN FAOI THALAMH, THE amazing World Under. This world consists of many large underground caverns with many passages connecting the caverns throughout the world. This guide will explain how the world works.

The first and greatest item needed for the World Under is water. There is an abundance of fresh water that comes from a massive oceanic river that follows the direction of Earth's equator, snaking north and south as it goes. It is one continuous belt. The river itself is an ocean deep, and its narrowest point is about 990 miles, or 1,600 kilometers. It takes on average three months for the water to float the whole way around Earth. The river's smooth current flows at an amazing speed. It is as if the river sits still as the World Under turns around it. The river connects six main continental caverns through various bays and seas, as well as many smaller caverns. The caverns are inner connected like a large sponge. There is more than enough fresh water for a world full of life.

The next important item for life below the crust is oxygen, which comes from the third important element for life: sunlight.

The oxygen and the sunlight are connected, stemming from the same source: the root systems. The root systems extend down through Earth's crust, coming from the largest forests and jungles on Earth's surface. They span the caverns and tunnels' ceilings. The forests and the jungles collect the sun's light and radiation and transfer them to the system below. The roots glow brightly during daylight hours and even give off a mild glow from the moon's reflective light. The roots also absorb carbon dioxide, replacing it with breathable oxygen.

With Earth on a tilted axis, rotating at the same time, we have a living world not just above but also below: a moving, living waterway; a living and breathing cavern ceiling; and warm days and cool nights. There is, on a hot, long day, enough light to evaporate water from the bays and rivers to create clouds and rainfall. The seasons above create the seasons below. When the earth above is having a hot summer day, it creates an annual rainy season below. The massive, moving oceanic river moves the seasons around the caverns under the surface. The World Under is beautifully lush, with an abundance of vegetation and animal life. The different-sized continental caverns and the angle of Earth's tilt led to the different seasons. Each cavern is unique, with its own ecosystem. It is an amazing world.

This guide has additional information for new travelers to take into consideration regarding what is in the World Under. There are also tunnels and caverns that are not properly mapped. Many are also not connected. Travelers can walk for miles and miles, fighting loops and flooding waters within tunnels that eventually turn into dead ends, or they might end up lost and never find their way back to civilization. Much of the Northern Hemisphere underneath the Arctic Circle is called the Uncharted Chambers. With little to no light and little water, it can be a confusing and dangerous place to be. Travelers in the uncharted territories need to remember there can be long stretches with little to no light. There also can be long areas with less oxygen, making it tougher and adding more of a physical toll in these areas. But there are travelers in the World Under who are better prepared. They prepare themselves with the right gear and use the uncharted territories for trading among the continental caverns. Most citizens in the world trade with one another through means of the waterway, the Great International River, the blood of the World Under, the belt of life.

All six of the main continental caverns have slightly different, unique social structures. The groups developed separately over time, at least until the last century slowly brought them together. Some of the cultures are semi-self-governed, but they are all subject to an international ruling party. The International World Under Senate is a lawmaking body put together by the monarchy of the World Under. This took place 600 years ago, after a long stretch of warring caverns. Since its establishment, there has been a good and enjoyable time of peace and growth. Each continental cavern gets to elect three senators as representatives. They get to voice their communities' concerns and opinions in the International World Under Senate. The Senators chose four Judges from their ranks to carry out the laws and rules of the communities of the World Under. The Senate works with all six continental caverns, and all four judges work together with all the caverns to ensure that all the communities' local leaders are conducting the World Under laws evenly and fairly over all the people. By having this ruling body in the World Under, the monarchy can spend its time and energy on the growth of trade and prosperity instead of many legal issues and local laws. The monarch's main strength is controlling the International Navy ensuring peace. This military presence deters and persuades all six caverns into maintaining peaceful trade and growth among all the different peoples.

To Banish a Tree

Trickery of a Magical Goat

RJ WYATT

CHAPTER 1

The Dance Begins

IT WAS A SUNNY DAY, AROUND TWO IN THE AFTERNOON, and the sun was at its highest point. There were three figures sitting just inside the entrance to a large cave. The cave ran deep into the center of the earth. A young girl sat quietly between two large men. All were staring across a large field dotted with half a dozen small trees. The girl could see a small stream on the far side. She looked at it with curiosity, also looking at the bright summer day with reverence.

Her captors, her guards, one on each side. Both were wearing leather armor with metal plates attached at various places. The leather was black to blend into the darkness. They carried short, curved swords. One of the guards kept rubbing his sword against the side of his boot. He would look at the other guard, then at the girl, and then back at the other guard. The second guard turned with a sideways glance at the first. The first guard said, "At least this one is being quiet."

The second guard replied, "I hate this kind of job, but at least it keeps us employed, and the closer we work with the Senate, the more money we make."

The young girl sniffed. They all stared into the bright sun. It was a hot, beautiful summer day. The first guard poked his boot again and said, "I wish the Senate Judge would hurry; it's mighty warm up here."

"It's not as if she's going anywhere soon," the second man replied. He laughed under his breath as he added, "She may not be going anywhere ever again." He looked at the girl. "Truthfully, it's up to the judge. You never know; you might be okay," he said with a nasty smirk on his face.

The girl sniffed again, trying hard not to let them see how upset she was. As they sat, they could hear footsteps echoing from far below. Both men stood to greet the far-off arriving guest. The sound continued, getting slowly louder and closer.

The girl looked away from the cave entrance, deep into the darkness. She could barely see the small glow of a lantern off to her side. The men also saw the lantern's glow.

The footsteps echoed around the chamber. They could see the silhouette of a figure. As the figure drew closer, the young girl realized it was a tall woman. The woman walked toward the men. She was two feet taller than the guards. And they were not small men. She wore a tall, pointed hat that only made her taller, the kind a witch or wizard would wear. She was a witch. She also was a Senate Judge, one of only four. The woman put a hand on the first guard's shoulder.

"Well, well, well, what have we here? Stand up, child," the tall woman commanded.

The girl looked up into the woman's face and slowly stood. She looked at the woman's outfit. She wore a long, velvety purple gown with gold streaks running through it, and the hat matched perfectly. On her shoulder was a fluffy black cat. It had a flat little face, and its tail twitched back and forth. The eyes were different. The girl had never seen a cat with purple eyes. She noticed the woman's eyes were purple as well.

Both men bowed slightly and addressed her as Your Honor.

"What is your name, child?" the judge asked, but the girl did not reply. "Come now. I don't have all day!"

"Me name is Abigail. Abigail Eberleaf." She was not just a girl; she was half human and half tree. She was thin and tall. Her skin was marbled with a mix of light green and grainy streaks of dark green. There were scales of bark on her shoulders, elbows, knees, cheekbones, and eyebrows. The bark was hard like the armor plating the guards wore but could flex like the dorsal fin on a dolphin. Her hair was not human hair; rather, vines as thick as pencils, with tiny leaves all down through them. The vines curled far down her back. She wore a multi-colored kilt mostly with greens that came down to the tops of her knees. Her top was a loose tank top with a flower at the end of the rainbow on the front. The shirt allowed her bark scales on her shoulders to move freely. She wore a thick belt with a small purse and short knife attached. On her feet, she wore brown leather boots that went up to the tops of her calves and laced up the front.

"You're surprisingly tall," the Senate Judge said. Abigail was just a couple of inches shorter than her guards. "How old are you, young lady?"

"I am ten, soon to be eleven," Abigail replied.

The judge cackled like a witch. "You know why you are here, young lady, don't you?"

Abigail shook her head no.

"That's surprising—playing dumb," the judge said. "Let me fill you in quickly because I don't have all day. You are here because you were caught with a torch—fire—in a forbidden area."

"I was looking for me parents," Abigail said.

"Silence!" the judge commanded. "It is good to hold your tongue. Not that it will matter because of what is going to happen to you. You had fire in a forbidden area. It does not matter what you were doing. All that matters is that you were caught there. It works quite well for me. You are being banished; you will be thrown into the field. It might as well be a death sentence. A young tree girl does not do well in the sunlight. Within the hour, you will start to root to the very spot where you stop. The sun will make you tired, and you will not be able to run forever. See those few trees out there in the middle of the clearing? They used to be just like you, and now they are nothing but trees."

"Do I not get a second chance, an opportunity to make it up?" Abigail pleaded.

"For most, a second chance probably would be granted. For you, the simple fact that you exist is the problem."

Abigail turned and tried to run, but before she even lifted a foot, she felt pressure on both shoulders as the guards grabbed her.

"Now, now, gentlemen. This one I shall enjoy!" the judge said.

The guards released their grip. Abigail took a step forward. Before she could take another, the judge spoke again, this time in the ancient language: "*Greimich.*"

Abigail felt pressure, as if the air itself were holding her in place. She looked at the witch, who was pointing at her with her magic wand. The witch slowly started spinning the wand in small circles. Abigail felt her body being pulled and pushed to turn around slowly toward the entrance of the cave. She stood looking out and heard the words of the witch behind her: "Run for the stream, child. At least there you will be able to quench your thirst for the rest of your life. Run as hard and as fast as you can, and maybe you will make it." The witch stopped circling her magic wand and, with the flick of her wrist, said another ancient word: "*tilgealh.*"

Suddenly, Abigail was thrust out of the cave and into the sunlight. She could hear the witch and the guards laughing behind her. She turned back toward the cave entrance but thought better of it. She turned and ran for the stream. Out of the corner of her eye, she spotted a patch of shade on a hillside just in front of a low cliff to the right of the valley—her chosen path. She changed direction and put on a burst of speed. She could feel the sun scorching her skin. It felt as if needles were pricking her from the inside out. Abigail pushed herself with all her might. Though she was beginning to feel extremely tired, she kept running for the shade on the hillside.

She dived into the shade and spied a small crevice up and to the left, under the cliff overhang but still inside the edge of the shade. It looked like a small cave. Abigail climbed with renewed energy and, using the last of her remaining strength, pulled herself inside. She had gotten out of the sun. She had made it! Abigail was not going to become rooted in this field today. The cool, dark air felt like icy-cold water running across her arms.

From behind her, she heard a small, squeaky voice ask, *Squeak, Squeak,* "Can I help you?"

As her eyes adjusted to the darkness, she could make out the silhouette of a small black bat. "I am just trying to get away from the sun," Abigail blurted out. "I have been banished from the World Under. That witch banished me to become a common tree in that field forever! All I wanted was me parents. They have been taken with the rest of our clan. I was out delivering tomatoes for me parents, and when I returned home, all I found was a note. The note said to go deep into Appalachia and get meself far away from the cities. It said they will always love me and told me not to look for them but to save meself. But I did not listen. I tried instead to find them. I was found and caught inside a tunnel. I had taken a torch mounted to the side of a wall and started me search. Some local villagers cornered me, yelling and screaming at me, asking me why I had fire. Before I knew it, they grabbed me and called for the local town guard. The next thing I knew, I was handed over to Senate guards and taken to be judged. The guards took me up to the cave entrance. I was told a judge from Appalachia would come explain how I could work off me punishment. But she did not explain. She banished me and chucked me out into the sun!"

Abigail took a deep, calming breath. "I am truly sorry. Am I allowed to be here? I cannot go back out there. I need to stay here, out of the sunlight."

Squeak. "I don't get many visitors," stated the bat. "My name is Squeaks."

Abigail looked at Squeaks for a few moments. As her eyes adjusted to the darkness, she saw that Squeaks was not very tall. She only came up to the bottom of Abigail's kilt. She had fluffy brownish-black fur that was shiny and curly. Her eyes were as black as her fur. She had a little scrunched-up pink nose, and she kept sniffing the air.

"I'm more than happy to have company. You did wake me up, though. This is normally when I'm sleeping. Up here on the surface, I sleep during the day and fly at night. There is a lot more food up here."

Her comment made Abigail realize that Squeaks too was a creature from the World Under.

Abigail made a somewhat unpleasant face at the idea of what dinner might be for her new friend. "I do not feel very well," Abigail said to Squeaks. "I think the sun really did hurt me insides."

Squeaks pointed to a dark corner. *Squeak, Flutter, Squeak,* "Go sit over there. It's darker. I'll go get you some water. I'll be right back."

Squeaks fluttered over to a coatrack, picked up a hat, and walked over to the cave entrance. She stretched her wings up and slowly let them fall as she scratched her back against the cave wall. "I'm itchy, *squeak,* today," Squeaks complained to herself as she licked at her arms. Out the door she darted.

As Abigail made her way over to the dark corner, she stopped and looked around the room. Squeaks had little shelves going up one wall. On the shelves were all sorts of dishes and pots. They were kind of funny looking, most likely made by Squeaks herself. In the center of the back wall was a tiny table with no chairs. On it was another oddly shaped pot, with a couple of flowers in it. She also saw a glass, a spoon, a knife, and a fork beside another oddly shaped plate.

Just off the entrance was a little coatrack where two more little hats hung. They were like the one Squeaks had grabbed on her way out the door. Abigail turned and made her way to the dark corner. She was still shaking.

Within a few minutes, Squeaks was back with a hat-ful of water. "Don't mind the hat; you can drink right out of it. I only wear it on weekends." *Squeak.*

Abigail looked at the hat and hesitated for a second. She was thirsty, and it really didn't matter. She drank all the water right down.

Squeaks went out for more, filling the hat to the brim.

Abigail chuckled and drank again. "I feel much better. Thank you very much. I am Abigail. Abigail Eberleaf. I am very pleased to meet you."

"It's a pleasure to meet you, Abigail," said Squeaks. The two looked at each other. "I do need to go back to sleep. The guards typically sit at the cave entrance for two or three days and then go back down the tunnel. Then we can return to the World Under. I will help you, if you don't mind having company. I will keep getting you water as you need, but I desperately need to get back to sleep. When I wake up, we can talk some more." Squeaks crawled up the wall; flipped upside down; and, within just a few minutes, went right to sleep, snoring lightly.

Abigail thought. *I truly could not have gotten any luck-ier than I am right now, I easily could have gone in the wrong direction. I would have become a stationary tree in the valley.* She said aloud, "Thank you," to no one in particular.

CHAPTER 2

Grandma and Grandpa's Farm

Grandma, Grandpa, and the twins had returned home late that night due to the twins' middle school orientation for sixth grade. The family had an opportunity to meet with their teachers and receive their books and class schedules. Grandpa kissed each of the twins and went right to bed. Grandma warmed up some apple tarts she had made earlier in the day from an old family recipe. She added a scoop of vanilla ice cream to each tart and gave them to the twins. After they finished their treat, Grandma followed the twins upstairs and tucked them into their beds. Even though the twins were ten years old, soon to be eleven, they still enjoyed being tucked into bed. Grandma made a special routine of it. She would pretend to be a witch waving and pointing a short magic wand around. She would look underneath their beds, in their closets, and out the windows, pretending to look for monsters. Grandma even made up and used odd words.

Grandma was soft-spoken and as sweet as her tarts. She was a tiny woman with black hair and bright blue eyes. She spoke with a slight German accent. She always chose bright colors for her sundresses, saying, "You always have to brighten things up." Her complexion was fair, and she had rosy cheeks on her little round face. Grandma was getting older, and it had become harder to keep up with the twins. There was always plenty of work to do around the farm. To stay in shape, her favorite hobby was gardening. They really didn't need to farm as much as they did, because they had plenty of money. She and Grandpa had taken in the twins when they were just tiny babies.

Grandpa was very much like Grandma. He had the same light complexion but a longer face, with a little dimple in the center of his chin. He had thinning blond hair and the greenest of eyes. He was still quite strong despite his age. Taking care of the livestock was the biggest thing he did on the farm. They had about two dozen cows and quite a few chickens. Grandpa even had a special goat named Paul, who had been around the farm for as long as the twins could remember. Grandpa dressed in denim overalls, leather work boots, and a ball cap when working around the property.

Grandma decided not to wake Grandpa, so she laid down on the sofa.

The next morning, Grandpa got up early. He needed to run into town to get some lumber. They had been having a problem with a hawk that kept eating their chickens. He wanted to build a new chicken coop that would better protect them. He woke Grandma on his way out to the barn.

Grandma yelled up the steps for the twins. She waited to see if she could hear them. They didn't respond. She listened for another minute. There was no commotion. After she had taken care of some household chores, an hour had passed. She needed to get the twins moving, or they would be late in getting to the fair. The county fair was held the second week of August every year. It was a big deal for the Meyer family. Today was to be the first day of the fair, setup day.

Grandma climbed the stairs to wake the twins, as she had many times. "You need to get a move on," she stated as she opened Miranda's door. She noticed that Aaron had climbed into Miranda's bed. He and his sister had a habit of climbing into each other's bed. They were monozygotic twins, identical but opposite genders, exceedingly rare. She did not think much of the habit, because they had always slept in the same bed as little children. But the twins were starting to get older, and that was not proper behavior for boys and girls. She shook her head. Grandma worried Aaron must have had another bad dream or seen more of his shadows, as he used to call them when he was younger. It amazed Grandma how much the two could agitate each other. But on the other hand, spend all their time together. She muttered under her breath and then said, "Get up! You don't need to be this lazy and sleep all day! Aaron, you are in the wrong bed. I will have breakfast ready and on the table in fifteen minutes. You two need to get a move on."

Miranda seized her opportunity; she popped out of bed and ran for the bathroom. Aaron, as always, realized a moment too late that he would get the bathroom second. The odds were that he would be lucky if he got any of the sausage from breakfast.

The twins' complexion was remarkably like Grandma and Grandpa's, but there were a few differences. They had a little more color. Both children had hair a deep reddish shade, and both had freckles on their cheeks. Grandma and Grandpa didn't have either of those traits.

A few years ago, Grandpa had dressed the kids identically. He would put Miranda's hair up under a ball cap. Even Grandma had not been able to tell the difference between the two. Even their freckles were almost in the same spots. Grandpa could tell them apart, though. Aaron had a small freckle on the bottom lobe of his left ear. In the last year, Miranda had grown an inch taller. She would tease Aaron about it. Aaron was starting to mature as well. He was stronger than his sister, spending plenty of time helping Grampa with the chores around the farm.

"Are you done in the bathroom yet?" Aaron shouted. "Hurry up, Miranda! I have to pee! I really mean it! If I don't get in there soon, I'll have to head out back! And you'd better not stink it up!" Aaron could smell sausage cooking now.

Miranda did not reply. *Click.* The door swung open. She shot past Aaron and down the stairs. "I'll save you two sausages!" she hollered back.

Aaron was halfway through the door. *Sheesh,* he thought as he fought with the string on the front of his pajama pants. *Life isn't fair.*

A few minutes later, Aaron joined his sister at the table. He was wearing a pair of jeans and a button-up denim shirt like Grandpa's, with a muscle shirt underneath. Miranda wore a pair of jeans. She and Grandma had spent plenty of hours bedazzling them. They had butterflies on the rear pockets and stars and moons all over them. She had on a button-up shirt that was tied in the front, with the sleeves rolled up and a pink t-shirt underneath.

Grandma set a plate down in front of Aaron. It had only a piece and a half of sausage.

"Sheesh," said Aaron. "Not even two." Miranda just smiled. Grandma set another plate down for Grandpa at the end of the table. It too had a piece and a half of sausage on it, as well as plenty of eggs. Just then, they heard the screen door slap. *Bang!*

Grandpa came in and sat at the end of the table. He handed Grandma an empty plate. "Paul ate that one right down."

Aaron's eyes got really big. "So now we are feeding Paul all the good sausage too?"

"Mind your manners. We always feed Paul," Grandma snapped.

Miranda asked the same question she had asked so many times before. "Why does Paul eat people food?"

Grandma looked at her through squinted eyes. "You are just like your brother."

Grandpa spoke up. "Paul is my buddy. I've known him since I was a kid."

"You mean you've had him since he was a kid," Grandma said quickly. Grandpa didn't reply.

"We will be enjoying the fair this week, and then you kids can get to go back to school in a couple of weeks. Are you ready?" Grandpa seemed excited about the fair this year. Paul was going, but he wasn't being shown. Grandpa was going to judge the goats this year, and he was looking forward to it.

The county fair was located not far from home. Now that the twins were older, as long as they stayed together and got along, they were permitted to have the run of the entire fairgrounds, including one concert of their choosing.

"As soon as you kids finish eating, we will load Paul and head toward the fairgrounds. I'm going to hook up the horse trailer now," Grandpa said.

Paul was an enormous old goat. He was, as goats went, larger than most. He weighed in at 327 pounds, a record breaker. He had a creamy white coat with a large blackish brown splotch in the center of his back. The splotch was in the shape of a large heart. His horns curled in a complete circle. Paul was not fat. He was all muscle.

"First, I have to get the lumber out of the truck. I want you to go see if Paul is in the barn or out in the pasture. I told him to be ready this morning," Grandpa said.

As if goats can understand you, Miranda thought.

"After I unload the lumber, I'll back the trailer up to the barn. If you have him in there, it will save us some time since we're already running a little late," Grandpa said as he picked up the old flannel shirt off the back of his chair and put it on over his white T-shirt.

Grandma picked up the twins' plates, even though Aaron was only half finished. He was able to snatch the last half sausage before it was gone. Grandma shooed them out the back door. The twins headed toward the barn.

Miranda turned to Aaron. "I'll race you!" She took two quick steps and said, "Go!"

Aaron bolted for the barn. Miranda had pretended she was going to run but just kept walking. She got to the barn, and Aaron stood there huffing and puffing. She smiled. "You'll surely stink now."

Aaron stuck his nose in his armpit. "I don't smell nothing," he said.

Miranda rolled her eyes. "You don't smell *anything*. Some days I wonder how you can be my twin."

Aaron pointed. "Paul's right there." As he opened the gate, his denim shirt caught a nail in one of the beams. *Rip.* "Man! I'm going to be in trouble!" He kicked a chicken's water feeder across the barn floor.

"How mature. Really."

Both twins spun around and looked at Paul. Paul looked back at them with his oddly shaped goat eyes. Then he just walked past them.

Aaron pointed at Miranda and then at Paul. "I know you heard that, Miranda."

Miranda looked at Aaron. She shook her head. "Nope. Just like the shadows you see—they don't exist. And even if I did hear something, I wouldn't give you the satisfaction."

Aaron started to get irritated. Just then, Grandpa opened the barn door. Paul walked out into the yard and up into the trailer. Aaron showed Grandpa the tear in his shirt. Grandpa shook his head and said, "If you hurry, maybe Grandma won't catch you."

Aaron ran past Grandma on the way to the house. Grandma jumped into the truck with Grandpa and Miranda. Aaron was back in a second, and then the truck was off. They pulled out of the driveway and turned to the right. A red car passed them going slowly in the other direction. In another couple miles, after they had made it on to State Route 11 heading north, a black SUV passed them going south, away from the fairgrounds. The driver seemed to look at their truck as if he were looking for something, but he kept on driving. Miranda noticed him. He was an oddly shaped man wearing some kind of fancy coat. She elbowed Aaron, but he just shook his arm as if to say, "Don't bother me."

The group didn't realize that the driver of the SUV didn't continue driving. He managed to cross the median, turn around, and follow them. After a little while, the SUV passed Grandpa. The driver then slowed a little, allowing Grandpa to pass him. Then the man sped up until he was side by side with the truck, speeding down the highway. Miranda looked at the man again, and he looked at her. He smiled, and then—*WHAM!*—he pushed their truck right off the edge of the road, trailer and all.

The truck slid down an embankment and then hit a tree. Grandma hit the windshield. The kids found themselves on the floor, squished up against the back of the front seat. Grandpa got up after a couple of minutes and realized Grandma was bleeding badly. He checked the twins, and they seemed okay. He ran around to the passenger side of the truck and had to force the door open. Grandma was not doing well. She was having problems breathing.

Miranda noticed the SUV was sitting up at the edge of the road, not far from where they were. The man got out of the SUV and started to walk toward the truck, when suddenly, there were sirens and red and blue flashing lights. Apparently, an officer coming up the highway had seen the accident. The man ran back to his SUV and took off.

The officer stopped and asked Grandpa if he was okay. Grandpa said, "Yes, but Grandma is hurt." The officer said he had already called in an ambulance, and it would be there in minutes. He asked if they would be okay until the ambulance arrived. Grandma nodded and raised a hand in a gesture to say okay. The officer took off after the SUV.

It wasn't long before the ambulance arrived. While it seemed to take an hour, it was only five minutes or so. Grandpa went around the back of the horse trailer. He opened the door, and Paul stepped out. Grandpa had put a small harness on Paul earlier, attached to a little leash. The paramedics were working on getting Grandma out of the truck and onto a stretcher.

Grandpa asked Miranda and Aaron if they had seen the man driving the SUV. Miranda described an odd-looking man with a long nose who wore a weird purple coat. He had jumped out of the SUV but then climbed back into it just as the officer arrived.

Grandpa spoke with Paul. "If I'm correct, we have been found. And Grandma is hurt badly. She hit her head good back there. Are you all right, Paul?"

Paul spoke for the first time in front of Grandpa and the twins. The goat's comment in the barn had not been a figment of the twins' imagination. Paul said, "I am fine, but the twins are in danger if you are correct."

Grandpa looked back down the road.

"That officer does not stand much of a chance. I hope he does not catch up to that SUV," Paul said. "We cannot be that far from the farm if we cross a couple fields."

"I agree," said Grandpa. "I'm going to go with Grandma in the ambulance. I'll catch up to you as soon as I can."

"I will take the twins back to the house and gather some supplies," responded Paul. "Then I will take them to Sabatini's Boots. We can use their entrance. We will meet you at that old goat's house," Paul added with some disgust, muttering under his breath.

Sabatini's Boots was owned by an energetic middle-aged man named Jimmy. Jimmy, his wife, and their three kids ran the business, making boots and selling them to the public. Grandpa always bought his work boots from Jimmy.

"I have to make sure Grandma is okay," Grandpa told the twins. "I don't have time for your questions right now. I wish I could answer them now, but I must go! Now, you do everything Paul says. He is in charge, so listen to him! I love you both very much. Paul, I am sorry. I have failed you," Grandpa said as he turned to hurry up the embankment and into the ambulance.

Aaron acted as if he wanted to say something. He looked as if he were on the verge of tears. Miranda spoke first. "Is Grandma going to be, okay?"

"I do not know," Paul answered. "I just do not know."

CHAPTER 3

The Second Stranger

P AUL SPOKE QUICKLY. "WE NEED TO HURRY! OUR friend will be back soon."

Aaron looked at Paul. "How can you talk?"

Paul replied, "Do not be daft, laddie. You think I am a real goat? I am a wizard! Now, let us get out of here before the Croatoan druid returns!"

"What's a Croatoan druid?" Aaron asked.

"Okay," Paul replied, "I will answer this one question to save meself aggravation. Think of a witch or wizard like a samurai. A druid is like an evil witch or wizard who is like a ninja. One would gladly stick a knife in your neck when you are asleep. They have no honor. We do not have time for any more questions, laddie. Miranda, take this leash off me; I do not want to get it caught on any brush. We will need to go down through the brush and up the other side of the ravine to leave the highway. There we can head across the fields and be back at me farm in thirty to forty minutes. Let us get a crack on; we need to do this before our druid friend shows back up!"

Miranda undid the leash, folded it up, and put it in her pocket. The three of them set out, and the twins tried to keep up with Paul. The group crossed one field and then the next. Paul stopped a couple of houses down from the farm and waited.

Paul pointed out, "There is a car in the driveway. We are going to have to sit here for a little while. Hopefully our unwanted guest will leave."

After what seemed like forever, the sun reached its highest point in the sky. Aaron asked Paul, "Do you think Grandma's going to be okay?"

Paul looked at Aaron. "Sure, she is going to be just fine." Then he frowned. "Okay, the truth is almost always better. Aaron, Miranda, I have no clue how your grandmother is going to do. All we can hope for is the best. She has always been very strong. Your grandmother also has your grandfather with her. She was a heck of a witch in her younger days."

Miranda just blinked at Paul.

"Grandma? A witch?" Aaron asked.

"Yes, and a very good one. Your grandpa not so much, but he made up for his lack of magical ability with his cunning wit. Strategically, he was one of me best lieutenants," Paul said. "Shhh! I see something. So, he has mates helping him."

A tall man came out of the back of the house and walked around to the front, where he had parked. He had something small in his hand. They heard two small cracks, almost like the sound of a .22-caliber gun going off. There was a flash of light in front of the farmhouse at the same time.

"Dirty rotten rat," said Paul. "I hope that was not me magic wand."

The stranger got into his car, backed out of the drive, and drove down the road toward the place where the accident had happened.

"I wonder how many of them there might be. We did get lucky. If they had caught us in the middle of the night, we would have been in big trouble."

"What was that flash of light?" Aaron asked.

"The Croatoan druid found two of our magic wands and snapped them. We must get into the house and get a few items. Me magic wand is kept in a wooden box on the fireplace mantel. There is a rose carved into the top of the box."

Aaron lifted his head, "I know the box you are talking about. Grandma said it belonged to our great-great-grandpa."

Paul shook his head. "No, it is me box. I carved it. Me magic wand is kept inside. Okay, I do not see the car coming back. Let us hurry!"

The group hurried across the road and into the farmhouse. Paul directed, "Both of you grab your school bags."

The twins looked at each other but did as he asked.

"Open them up. You will not need schoolbooks where you are headed, at least not that kind."

Miranda smiled as she flopped her books down into the sink on top of some dirty dishes. Aaron looked into his bag and then back at Miranda. He carefully set his books on the kitchen table, as if they were prized possessions. He acted insulted at how Miranda had treated such objects.

"Okay, both of you upstairs. Grab two sets of clothing each, and do not forget your underwear and toothbrushes."

The twins hurried upstairs.

"And pajamas! And do not take all day!" Paul yelled up the stairs. "We still have to get a couple more things before we go."

"Go where?" Aaron yelled down the steps.

"To the old goat's house, like I said earlier."

"Whose house?" Miranda asked.

"Me cottage. One of the few safe places we can go—well, safe for some."

"What do you mean?" Aaron asked.

"Just gather your crap and get down here!" Paul yelled, stomping his foot impatiently.

"Why do I need a toothbrush?" Aaron asked.

"Because you do not want to be using me tooth-brush," Paul replied.

There was silence for a moment. "Good point," the twins said in unison.

"Miranda, go get me box on the fireplace."

She did as he said.

"Aaron, go down to the basement, and grab one of Grandpa's hammers off the workbench. Grab a couple bottles of water too."

Aaron hurried back with the hammer and the water.

"Now set the box on the floor, on its side. Aaron, hit the box with the hammer, not too hard but not too soft. Like breaking an egg open but not breaking the yolk. We do not want to break me magic wand inside."

Miranda asked Paul, "Why don't you just open it?" Aaron rolled his eyes.

Paul shook his head, "I know Aaron gets the good grades, but I figured everyone in this room would know why. Does it look like I have thumbs? It is a trick box, and it would take hours to explain how to open it."

Aaron did as he was asked. He hit the box twice, crushing in the side. Out rolled a long greenish black magic wand with a few streaks of silver. The tip was deep red. Halfway down the shaft, it had dark green thorns. The base of the handle was a dark brownish black, shaped like the bottom of a flower bulb. It was shorter than a conductor's wand, like ones used in a schools marching band. The magic wand was not sleek and elegant like grandmas.

"Miranda, I want you to carry that."

Just then, they heard car tires crunching on the gravel again. Aaron peeked out the side window. "It's that car again!"

"Okay, everybody to the basement."

The group moved quickly to the basement. They could hear the man come in the back door. "I know you's in here. I see books in a sink," the man called out in a raspy voice. They could hear his boots tapping on the floor, and every so often, a board would squeak. They heard him climb the stairs.

Paul pointed his nose toward the storm door, "It is now or never. We will use the basement stairs out to the yard."

The group pushed up and opened the old wooden basement door. Then could hear the man's footsteps coming down the stairs. He must have heard them.

Paul directed, "I want you kids to run along the fence toward the woods. Let us get a move on it!"

The three of them started running down the side yard. Paul stopped. The twins ran a few more feet and then stopped. Paul hollered at the twins, "I did not say to stop!" The twins trotted on, but they kept looking back.

Paul dropped his head horns first, leaned into a full-tilt boogie, and sprinted back toward the house, toward the basement stairwell. Just as the man emerged — *wham!* — Paul drove his horns into the chest of the stranger. Both went flying down the basement steps.

Aaron stopped instantly. Miranda took only a few more steps. There was a sickening, loud thud. Within half a minute, Paul emerged. He ran toward the twins. "I told you not to stop!" He sprinted past them. "Follow me."

As they reached the tree line, the group slowed to a brisk walk. Paul was now slightly limping. "I hit him good. He's out cold. Whether we have got thirty minutes or two hours, I do not know. We cleared all the steps. The druid's head hit the ceiling beam and then bounced off the floor when he landed on his back. I can only hope I killed him. I also bruised me knee." Paul explained.

"We are going to head south, where there is an entrance to the World Under. It is in the back of a store, Sabatini's Boots. In fact, Grandpa should have had Jimmy keep a few emergency supplies for me there. We will get there close to early evening. It will take up a three- to four-hours for us to walk there. We need to get there before Jimmy closes his shop at six o'clock." Paul stated the plan.

Aaron started to say, "Will Grandpa know—"

Paul cut Aaron off. "Grandpa knows right where I am going. You are supposed to be the smart one." Paul shook his head again.

Miranda laughed. "I'm liking you more and more," she said to Paul.

"Why? Because I am a troublemaker like you?"

Miranda's laughter stopped. Her smile turned into half a frown. But Aaron was smiling now.

The group picked up their pace as they set out for Sabatini's.

CHAPTER 4

The Party Goes Underground

THE GROUP MADE IT TO SABATINI'S BOOTS JUST before closing time. Jimmy and his wife, Joyce, took them inside. Jimmy thought it would be best if Paul stayed downstairs in the shop. Jimmy and Paul remained downstairs, discussing the situation. The twins were ushered upstairs by Joyce. Miranda heard the conversation between Paul and Jimmy as she slowly climbed the stairs.

"I hope I killed him, Jimmy!"

"But you said there were two!" Jimmy replied.

"Take this stupid harness off me back, and yes to the earlier question. Of course, I am housebroken," said Paul, sounding insulted.

The dinner Joyce fixed was good: macaroni and cheese with sausage and green peas mixed in. After dinner, Joyce escorted the twins to her son Michael's room. "I'm going to put you two up here for the night. Michael hasn't come home yet. He's been out doing some running around. He can stay with his sisters Rachael and Kristin. You two can have his room. Tomorrow is going to be a big day, and you need to get some sleep. We're going to see what we can find out about your grandmother and grandfather. I'll make a phone call to the hospital in the morning after we all have our breakfast, to see how your grandma is doing, alright."

The twins hated being treated like little children. With all that was going on, there wasn't a lot they could do about it. Miranda went over to the bed and flopped down. It had been a long day, and there was a lot to take in. Aaron sat at the end of the bed, poking at Miranda's shoes. She kept ignoring him. Finally, she snapped, "Aaron stop! Lie down and get some sleep."

Aaron flopped down onto the bed beside her. She was staring at the ceiling. It was a neat little room, with all sorts of ribbons all over the walls—awards won by the Sabatinis' son. There was a computer over on the far desk, and model airplanes hung from the ceiling. It was a typical boy's room.

"I hope Grandma is okay," said Aaron. "This is just crazy."

Miranda rolled over and put a hand on Aaron's shoulder. "She'll be fine," she said, not knowing if that was true. A tear rolled down her cheek. She was always the strong one, so she didn't say a word.

Before the twins fell asleep, they heard Jimmy come upstairs. He was talking to his wife in the hall just outside their son's room. Jimmy said, "I never thought I'd see the day. The royal twins in our home."

"They came into the shop once with Edward," Joyce said. "They have no clue who they really are?"

"Not a clue," replied Jimmy. "Well, let's get to bed so we can see them out in the morning bright and early. Paul's standing guard. Who would have thought — Paul, a goat? I thought Edward was pulling my leg. One of the most gifted wizards reduced to being a goat. Paul pointed out that our passage is not necessarily a secret. We should expect visitors, and we should probably close shop and move back down below or move somewhere safer up here."

Joyce sounded worried, "Jimmy we are probably a sitting target if a druid is involved."

Jimmy replied. "We'll talk more about the plans in the morning, dear. I've had all I can take. This is truly going to change our lives for a little while."

The next morning, when the group got up, Jimmy cooked a large breakfast. Everyone ate his or her fill. Paul had plenty of eggs. He turned to Jimmy and said, "Not baaaaad." The Sabatinis, Paul, and the twins burst out laughing.

It was almost time for the shop to open. Jimmy heard a knock at the door. He went down to look. It was a customer, one of his regulars, Mr. Leaper. Jimmy noticed a black SUV in the far corner of the parking lot. Normally, he would have let the customer into the shop even though it was still ten minutes till opening time, but because of the SUV, he wrote a note and showed it to his customer: "I'm sick today and not opening the shop." He knew he only had a few minutes. As the customer returned to his car, Jimmy rushed upstairs, yelling as he went, "We've got to move now! One of the Croatoan druids is outside in the parking lot. The only reason he hasn't stormed the door is because there was a customer out front, Mr. Leaper, who is now leaving."

"We do not have much time," Paul said. "Everyone, grab your bags and hurry downstairs."

"Honey, take our kids, and go! Go north to your cousin's house," Jimmy told Joyce. "We will use one of the northern entrances and head toward Boston. I won't be far behind."

Joyce hurried their kids out the back door of the shop and into a station wagon. They headed north.

Jimmy showed Paul and the twins where the ladder was located. "We only have a minute or two!"

Just then, the group heard another knock on the front door. It was more of a bang. Someone desperately wanted into the shop. The twins hurried down the ladder with their school bags. Jimmy threw a set of saddlebags over Paul's back and buckled them on. Then he lowered Paul down with a rope. Paul and the twins looked up at Jimmy. Jimmy just smiled. "I worked my whole life to build this business, and I'm going to go out with a bang! I need you three to run as hard and as fast as you can. Get as far down the tunnel as possible." Jimmy pulled up the ladder. He then held

up what looked like a large road flare and shook it in his hand. "Hurry now."

The group heard the trap door slam shut. Then the front door crashed in. A man demanded, "Where are you hiding those brats!"

"Wouldn't you like to know!" Jimmy shouted.

Then he must have lit the dynamite.

Paul caught on quickly. He pushed the kids. "Run! Dynamite! Run!!!"

Miranda and Paul moved quickly, and Paul pushed Aaron as he went. Aaron was trying to go back. The explosion was deafening. The roof of the tunnel shook, and the ground moved beneath their feet. The light bulb beside where the ladder once stood disappeared under a pile of rubble and a cloud of dust. "That should at least give us safe passage to the old goat's house. At least we will not have the druid on our tail," said Paul.

"I hope Mr. Sabatini got out of there," Aaron said.

"We will find out more news when we get to one of the bigger cities like Boston in a couple of days. It is going to take us a while," said Paul.

Miranda asked, "What do you mean by *Boston*?"

Paul explained, "Well, there is a World Under Boston, underneath the surface Boston, in our world. Come to think of it, it is not really that far from the one above—almost straight below."

"I can't see," Aaron interrupted.

"That makes sense," Paul replied. "You have lived above ground for so long that your eyes do not properly work. Just close your eyes for a few minutes. Maybe they will work a little better."

Miranda and Aaron did as Paul suggested. After a few minutes, they both could see somewhat. They could make out their own hands and could see each other's silhouette.

"Can you see your hands?" Paul asked.

"Slightly," replied Miranda.

"Both of you, come toward the sound of me voice," Paul said. "I do not need you walking into a wall or off a cliff. Your eyes should hold a little light for a few more minutes."

The twins worked their way toward the sound of Paul's voice humming some Irish tune.

"You are World Under born, and your eyes ought to be better in the dark than the eyes of those born in the world above."

They both climbed onto Paul's back.

"Do not get used to it," Paul pointed out. "I do not belong to you."

The group continued to descend into the darkness. After some time, Miranda noticed a line in the ceiling.

"Wow," Miranda stated.

Paul replied, "I keep forgetting how little you know. You really do not know anything about our world, do you? That faint line is not a line or a crack. It is the very tip of a root system. It will go on for hundreds of miles, and it will grow in size as the chamber grows. It is attached to a couple dozen of the great trees on the Appalachian Trail above. Those trees cycle light down to our world as well as give us oxygen. As the sun, above the surface, reaches its brightest and then dims in the evening, so does the root light. There will even be light with the moon's glow. There are vast caverns the size of continents down here. There are huge cavern systems beneath all the major continents above. Welcome to your world. Welcome to the World Under!"

CHAPTER 5

Paul Loses Aaron

A FTER A WHILE, THE GROUP STOPPED TO TAKE A break. Aaron walked away from Miranda and Paul. He was staring up at the line in the ceiling.

The root had grown wider and now had small branches stemming off of it. Miranda pointed out, "The root is getting brighter." The tunnel had grown to approximately twenty feet high and forty feet wide. The single root lit up the entire tunnel. There was a musty smell.

"This is amazing!" Aaron exclaimed.

Paul chuckled. "You have not seen anything yet, laddie. The world above is nothing compared to what is down here. The irony is that most of the surface dwellers do not even know it exists. The surface was a safe place for your grandma and grandpa to take you both."

"What did the Sabatini's mean when they referred to us as the royal twins?" Miranda asked as she and Paul approached Aaron.

"Well," Paul said, "you are not supposed to be ear-wigging into others' conversations. I did not want you to find out yet. I do not want you to talk to anybody you meet down here about who you really are. But I also do not think it really is going to matter that you know. We are being hunted because you are the last of the royal families left in the World Under. About thirty years ago, a really powerful group of wizards, druids, and a few witches, known today as the New Croatoan Order of Druids, this new group of druids decided they no longer wanted to be led by the royal families, that is to say, ruled by common nonmagical people. Most people down here are not magical, but those who are think they are above everyone else. To have common people, even though they are royalty, telling them what they are permitted to do is apparently a hard pill for them to swallow. There has been plenty of magic in the royal line. Your father's great-uncle Argyle was quite gifted. He was simply amazing. I knew him quite well when I was just a lad," smiled Paul.

"They, the New Croatoans, think they are above the law. Within ten years, they started hunting all the royal families and killing them off, one by one. Nobody knew exactly who was doing it. It turned out the traitors were some of the closest people to the royals. Before we knew it, the only family left was yours. Regarding what I tell you, some of it is known, and some is speculation on me part. I will stress me warning, again. It is not wise to share what I tell you as we meet new people in your new world. I was not going to tell you anything, because I figured we would be safer if you did not know about your past, but since you now know. Promise me you will not share that you are royals with others. The New Croatoan Order must have found out from a member of me old post. Probably a drunk guardsman not thinking or just bragging about your existence. I thought for sure I had erased every last ounce of proof that you had been saved," Paul explained.

He took a deep breath and then began again. "For about ten years, your parents were the only royals left. Then you two were born and the World Under seemed filled with joy. We believed we had managed to eliminate all those who had attacked the royal families in the past, or so we thought. The royal guard had a few wizards like meself. I was one of the guards' upper commanders. The captain of a fleet vessel which escorted the King and Queen around the World Under. Me ship sat near the entrance to Sagano, the Daintree Sea. This is one of the six continental caverns. It sits beneath the country of Japan. Me ship was one of two that oversaw escorting the King and Queens Royal Ship. Your parents had taken you to the embassy in upper Sagano to deal with some trade disputes between Sagano and Queensland. They had just arrived at the little embassy cottage. Your attendant took you to the nursery to give you dinner and play with you, as usual. The king and queen had to sit down to dinner with the representatives of Queensland as well as Sagano," Paul had their attention.

Paul hung his head, "Suddenly, there was an attack on the outer wall of the compound. Before the family knew it, the intruders had breached the wall and were burning the surrounding cottages. The embassy guards were outnumbered ten to one. Bats were sent out to deliver messages by the guard. The community did not have time to wait for their request for help to be answered. The embassy guard was a small, select group of fighters. They bought everyone as much time as they could. The diplomats realized they were on their own as well, and it was going to be a fight for their lives. The attackers were too powerful. They destroyed most of the compound, looking for any and all ambassadors, representatives, and your royal family. Many fought back with your father. Your mother quickly rushed to the nursery. She wrapped both of you into a small picnic basket. She had a large bat take you just outside the northern wall. I am sure her intent was to catch up with you there." He took a deep breath.

Paul was staring up into the glow of the roots light. He seemed to be speaking more to himself now, "Like most in the compound, your parents never made it. Their cottage was made of wood—bamboo. The New Croatoan Order burned everything and killed everyone they encountered. The druids must have seen the bats leave earlier, because they did not wait around. A bat dropped onto the deck of the ship I oversaw and delivered a note to one of me soldiers. Me ship was the closest, but by the time I and me troops got there, there was nothing left. The place was totally engulfed in flames, and there was not a soul to be found. We worked for hours to put out the flames. I found your father's crown meself. At that point, I sent a messenger to inform the International World Under Senate, a kind of union of all the governing continental caverns. I think we were all in shock. I sent most of me troops back to their posts on the ships. A little old lady found one of me guardsmen and hand-delivered the picnic basket to him. He brought it to me."

Aaron spoke up. "So that's why we were sent to live with Grandma and Grandpa." Miranda just looked at him and didn't say a word.

Paul looked at the twins and realized he had said too much. He stood up quickly. "Well, let us get moving. We do not need to hang out here. I need to make it to the old goat's house."

As they moved farther down the tunnel, Miranda asked Aaron, "Do you hear something?"

The twins were riding on Paul's back again. He immediately stopped. They could hear faint shuffling behind them. It stopped when they did. Paul continued on and stopped again. Sure enough, they heard more shuffling, and again it stopped. Paul turned his head up and spoke into Miranda's ear. "I am going to try to lose them. We are definitely being followed. Me guess is somebody is hungry, and whether you realize it or not, down here, I am a delicacy." As the tunnel got larger and brighter, they could see in the distance behind them a half dozen rats. Unlike rats above ground, they were the size of large dogs. "Once we make it around the bend up ahead and I cannot see them anymore, I am going to drop you both off to the right. I will circle around and try to take out one or two. That ought to be enough to chase them away."

Paul dropped off the twins and then darted back toward the rats. The kids heard a squeal off in the distance and then another squeal. Then there was silence. Within a minute, they could hear Paul's hooves. He was coming fast.

Paul made the bend and caught up to the twins. "Miranda, Aaron, there are more than I thought. There were eight; now there are only six."

"Is that blood?" Aaron asked.

"Yes, but it is not me blood," Paul said. "But we'd better get ready because we are in for a fight."

Aaron stepped up beside Paul, squeezing his sister behind them.

"Wait," Paul said. "I have an idea. I do not know if it will work, but it is worth trying. Do you have me wand, Miranda?"

She dug through her school bag and pulled out the magic wand.

"I want you to point it down the tunnel toward where the rats are coming from. Point the wand at the rats when they come around the corner," Paul directed.

Miranda did as she was told.

"Close your eyes, and concentrate," Paul directed. "Picture a fire then say the word *tine*."

Miranda did as he asked. A tiny flicker of flame came from the end of the wand. That was all.

"Hand the wand to your brother."

Aaron tried next. *"Tine!"*

A black wisp of smoke shot from the end of the wand. This approach was not working. The rats were getting closer.

Miranda reached over and grabbed the wand from Aaron's hand. *"Tine!"*

This time, a line of flame ten inches or so emerged.

"That is a start," Paul said. "I will have to talk me way out of it."

Miranda put a hand on Paul's horn. Before she could say a word, Paul shouted, *"Tine!"*

There was an explosion of flames. A fireball shot straight down the tunnel, hitting two rats, driving them into the tunnel wall, and causing the rest of them to scatter.

"Lonrach (Brilliant), Well, I will be," Paul exclaimed. "I am not a useless goat after all. Let us get a move on before they regroup and retaliate. We have about a two day walk to get to the old goat's house."

The group walked on. Giving Paul a break, the twins walked beside him. Paul said, "Just so you know, you both did very well. I have never seen anyone else produce black smoke using the word for fire. You both have some abilities. I do not know which abilities."

Aaron looked a bit discouraged. "I see shadows. Sometimes they try to get my attention and talk to me. When I was little, they used to scare the heebie-jeebies out of me. Then I realized they couldn't hurt me."

Miranda interjected. "It's a bunch of rubbish."

Paul stopped in his tracks. "I am not exactly sure what it is, but it is not rubbish. You should be careful, Aaron, because they can hurt you."

Aaron looked a little worried.

Paul continued. "We do not know much about ghost shadows. They are thought to be an imprint of a soul left behind. The soul will have gone on. Like a leftover copy but not the soul. It is something I will have to put some research into. I am certain you should stay away from such creators. It is one of those gifts that witches and wizards of old have studied, but few really understand it. Most who study such topics are not sociable. Some even seem, or just are, crazy. Some of the ancient witches and wizards supposedly understood it, but it's one of those magical gifts that has somewhat died out. I would not tell anyone that you can see such things. Keep that to yourself." Paul shook his head "Talking to the dead."

They continued walking.

Toward the end of the day, the group found a small stream. There was plenty of light there, even though the sun must have been setting in the world above, as the glow of the roots was starting to fade. "This is probably not a bad place to spend the night," Paul said. "We can fill our water bottles from the farm, and we will have plenty of water for our walking tomorrow." The twins lay down and cuddled next to Paul.

The next morning, when the group got up and brushed their teeth, Aaron brushed Paul's teeth with a toothbrush that Paul had in the supplies from the saddle bags. Miranda made it clear that it would be a cold day, before she ever brushed Paul's teeth. It was going to be a long day for everyone. The group drank as much water as they could and then moved on.

There seemed to be little to talk about. The twins asked a few more questions about magic, but Paul seemed preoccupied and ignored them. After a while, Paul shook his head and responded, "That will be up to your school instructors, not me."

Miranda looked as if she were going to be sick to her stomach. *School? Down here?*

Paul continued. "Despite the fact that you so far have seen only a glowing root, some rats, and a stream, there is a whole world down here, with cities and ships. There are stores, restaurants, museums, and different countries. You will both be fine, and this is a good place for you." Paul smiled at Miranda.

Miranda uttered one word: "School." She let out a deep breath, puffing up her cheeks and blowing air up across her face, causing her bangs to flutter.

Aaron looked at her with a sympathetic gaze. "We are just kids," he said.

The group continued for a few hours. Eventually, they found a wall with mushrooms growing from floor to ceiling under a thicker spot in the root above. There was a sweet smell in the air. Paul tore off a chunk of mushrooms and started chewing. He looked at the twins and smiled. "Are you not hungry? Go ahead; they are harmless."

Miranda didn't try a bite at first, but Aaron ripped off a chunk and started eating. "Not bad, Sis. They really don't have much flavor, like popcorn or stale bread."

Miranda took a bite. "It's better than nothing in my stomach. You said they have restaurants down here?" she asked Paul.

Paul smiled. "The best. It has been a long time since I have been down here. Do not get me wrong. I do not mind bacon, eggs, and sausage. All that is good. But there is nothing like the eggplant parmesan in Pisa at Richie Retorts Italian Bistro and Winery. I hope it is still there."

Just then, the group heard more feet shuffling in the tunnel behind them. "Seems our friends have not quite given up," Paul pointed out. "I think they are curious as to where we are going. I do not expect them to attack again. It is one thing for a group of rats to attack a small group walking way out in the middle of nowhere; it is quite another to attack a small group out in the middle of nowhere with a skilled wizard among them. I think they are just trying to keep tabs on us. Maybe they can make a few copper bits by telling the right people what they have seen. Most rats are exactly that: rats."

Paul had the twins climb onto his back. "Let us give them a bit of a workout again." He broke into a heavy trot. "I figure I can keep this pace for a couple hours, at least till lunchtime. By then, they will be tired enough that they will not try anything stupid."

The group continued forward. By lunchtime, they found themselves back by the stream. The stream had gotten wider and faster. On the other side of them was a vast opening to another chamber below them. It was so dark they could not see the bottom. The group sat down and drank plenty of water. There was no sign of the rats yet.

"We had better play it safe," said Paul. "I do not think we are going to sleep this evening. I want to keep moving through the night. I do not want those creeps coming upon us in the dark."

Aaron needed to put his shoes back on. He had taken them off and was splashing his feet in the stream. Paul whispered in Miranda's ear. The two laughed.

Aaron squinted at them. "What's so funny?" he asked.

Miranda smiled and replied, "I don't know, but check your feet, and make sure you don't have any leeches."

Aaron's eyes got big. He yanked his feet out of the water, looking all over them. "What the heck is wrong with you? Why would you let me put my feet in the water?"

Paul just turned his head sideways. "Life lessons laddie. Sometimes life is best learned by experiencing it." Miranda laughed at her brother. Aaron looked irritated but said nothing.

Miranda started to move on. Aaron quickly pulled his socks and shoes on. Then he noticed the cliff. He walked over to the edge and looked down. It was more like a steady, gradual slide of loose rocks. The bottom was not visible. "Hey, Paul! There's no bottom!"

Paul turned and looked at Aaron. He quietly said, "I would like you to slowly turn around and come over here. You do not need to be that close to the edge."

Aaron spun around. His feet shot out behind him, and down he went.

Miranda sprinted over toward him, but Paul caught the back of her jeans in his mouth just in time. "No, I do not think so," Paul grunted out.

Miranda was screaming. "Aaron! Aaron, are you all, right?" Miranda and Paul stood there for a minute.

"I'm okay," Aaron called up. "I just can't see down here. All I can see is the glow from your tunnel."

"You stay right there!" Paul yelled. "Do not move!" Paul was torn. Should he risk Miranda? Should he risk himself? It was a wonder Aaron hadn't broken his neck, an arm, or a leg. "Just stay put! I am thinking."

It would take a day to get to the old goat's house. Then it would take Paul another day to make his way back up Aaron's tunnel. Aaron would just about die of lack of water. Paul's mind reeled at the conundrum he was facing. He heard some shuffling off in the distance. *Rats! I cannot leave Miranda and go over and down to get Aaron.*

Miranda asked, "Is there anything we can do?"

"I know only one thing I can do." Paul snorted. "I am going to kill the rats—the whole lot of them. I am going to smash them into oblivion!" Paul turned and looked back out over the cliff.

Squeak. Squeak. Amid flapping and squeaking, a voice said, "What can I do for you? And who is that boy down below?"

"Well, I will be a shish kebab!" Paul said.

"Oops, maybe I had better not say that, especially with the luck I am having today," Paul mumbled to himself.

"Well if I could see you I am sure you would be a sight for sore eyes. You blend into the dark quite well. Me name is Paul. To whom do I have the pleasure of addressing?" Paul requested.

"My friends call me Squeaks. Squeaks the bat," she giggled out.

"Definitely a pleasure," Paul said with joy.

Miranda spoke up. "About my brother—please don't eat him."

"Well, I wouldn't want to," Squeaks retorted.

Paul kicked at Miranda lightly. "Do not go," Paul begged. "She does not know what she is talking about. The boy is our young companion, Aaron. This is his sister, Miranda."

"They are almost identical," Squeaks said.

"Yes, they are," Paul replied. "You are very observant. They are identical twins—and a royal pain in me backside!"

Squeaks giggled. Miranda made a face.

"You see, I really need your help," Paul said. "There will be plenty of food in it for you. Are you familiar with where you are in the tunnel?"

Squeaks said yes.

"We have a problem. We are headed to a little cottage about a day from here. Do you know where that cottage is?"

Squeaks replied, "Yes, I think so. A skinny lady lives there."

"Why, yes," Paul said. "Can you take our young companion to the house?"

Squeaks shook her head. "I'm not sure. I'll have to check with my friend."

Paul looked at Miranda while Squeaks flew off. Within a few moments, she was back. "Abigail said okay, but she's not really in much of a people mood. She is quite hungry, though."

"Great," Paul said. "Squeaks, describe your friend for me."

"Kinda tall. Vines for hair," Squeaks said.

"So, she is an evergreen," replied Paul.

"Yes, that's what I said," Squeaks replied.

"Come here, Squeaks, and I will let you in on a personal secret of ours," Paul said.

Squeaks flew over and stood beside Paul. He leaned over and whispered in her ear. Squeak's eyes got huge. "We will definitely take good care of him. We'll see you at the house," Squeaks said.

Paul looked at Miranda. "Climb on, lassie. Let us make haste. We still have plenty of rats behind us."

Paul headed down the passage at a decent clip. Squeaks returned to her new friends down below.

CHAPTER 6

New Friends

SQUEAKS FLEW BACK TO ABIGAIL AND WHISPERED IN her ear, and the two of them walked to where Aaron stood. Abigail spoke first. "You must be Aaron. Me friend Squeaks here is a bat. She had a conversation with your goat. We are supposed to help you get to the cottage at the end of our path."

"Hey, you sound a lot like our goat. I would thank you. But I can only see your silhouette," Aaron replied.

"This tunnel probably does not get traveled much because it is so dark," Abigail said. "Squeaks here can see fine for all of us." Abigail carefully reached out and found the top of Aaron's head. She moved her hand down to his shoulder and then down to grab his hand. "When Squeaks says, 'Step high,' we step as if we are going to step over a large rock, because if we do not, we will trip over a rock. Are you okay holding me hand? If not, we can crawl. It might take a few days."

"That's okay," Aaron responded. Squeaks then grabbed Aaron's other hand, and the three set off.

"We'll get to some light in another hour or two if the sun is still up or the moon is out," Squeaks said.

It didn't take long. As they continued down the path, Aaron noticed the glow of a small root in the ceiling. He knew the moon was out.

Once the trio could see the shapes of their surroundings, they no longer had to hold hands. They all sat down on a large rock. Abigail rubbed her feet and arms. She was still dealing with sunburn. If you could call it that. It hurt more from the inside out. Aaron sat there staring. He couldn't take his eyes off Abigail. Abigail started to blush.

"It's rude to stare," Squeaks said.

Aaron looked down at his hands. "I'm sorry. I didn't realize," he muttered. He looked back at Abigail. "You're just not a person."

Abigail folded her arms. "I am so a person!"

"Well, not like any person I've ever seen," Aaron replied.

"Why are you staring at her?" Squeaks asked.

"She's different. She's kinda pretty. I don't know," Aaron answered.

Everyone fell silent, and then Aaron finally spoke up again. "I'm sorry. That was rude."

"It is okay," Abigail said turning away from Aaron. "'We are just going to rest here for half an hour because me feet are hurting. It has been a long couple of days for me."

Squeak, Squeak, "We will be at the little house some-time just after the midday light," Squeaks said. "We should meet your friends there at about the same time."

They sat there for a while. When their half-hour rest was over, they headed on down the path. Aaron kept stealing glances at Abigail. Abigail noticed but was now taking a different approach: she was ignoring him. Squeaks shared some mushrooms with Aaron, trying to distract him. The group kept moving down the path.

Aaron volunteered, "We came from the surface. Where are you from?"

Abigail hesitated. "I am from the western part of the Appalachian cavern." She said nothing of her parents.

"Well, I am from a farm just outside a little village in Ohio called Columbiana. But Paul says we are from down here. I'm not sure," Aaron said.

Squeaks interrupted. *Squeak, Squeak,* "So you are not a prince? The goat said you and your sister are royalty."

"I know he says that." Aaron said, "but I think Paul is a little touched in the head, maybe even crazy. He pretends to be some great captain of some royal navy. Nuts, I tell you. He's a goat."

Squeaks giggled. *Giggle, Giggle, Squeak, Giggle.*

Aaron thought to himself; *Everything seems like a dream. But Paul can also work magic and Grandpa was okay with him bringing us here.* "He brought us down here because there were bad men after us. He called them Croatoan druids. One of the men caused the auto acci-dent that our grandma was hurt in." Aaron stopped walking for a second and looked down at his feet. He could now barely make out the shape of them. "I just hope she's okay. All I want is my grandma to be okay."

The two girls stopped walking as well. As they turned and looked, they realized Aaron seemed like he was about to cry. The cavern had gotten a little brighter, and the group did not need to hold hands anymore.

Aaron said, "Grandma and Grandpa are all we have, and now I've lost my sister too. I don't have anybody."

Squeaks and Abigail came back to him. Abigail looked down at Aaron. "Right now, you have us. I know that is not a lot, but it is better than nothing. We can work together. I am looking for me family, and I do not exactly know what could be happening either. Cheer up. You know your sister has the goat."

Squeaks nodded. "She seemed okay when I saw her on top of his back."

Aaron gave a little smile.

Abigail said, "We can rest here for ten minutes. Me arms and legs still hurt." She went over and sat down on a rock.

Aaron turned to Squeaks. "You know, tomorrow is supposed to be Miranda's and my birthday. I hope to catch up to her. She is the biggest pain in the rear. She's impossible. I have never once been without my sister, even though she drives me bonkers. She's my best friend, my sis. She's like part of me, the other half of me. She seems to know what I'm thinking. We've always kind of been that way."

Abigail stood up and came back over. "I do not quite understand. One second you are saying how great she is, and the next second you are complaining she is a pain in your hind quarters." She looked at him sideways.

"Yup, that's it," Aaron explained. "We're identical twins. We used to trick our schoolteachers all the time. The only one who ever seemed to get it right was Grandpa. And he wouldn't tell us how. I hope we catch up to Miranda early in the morning. This will be the first night I have ever been without her. And like I said, tomorrow's our birthday."

"Me birthday is in March," Abigail said. "I am a March tree. You do not get much earlier than that. Well, there are a few who have been born in February, but it is very rare."

Aaron asked, "Why is that?"

"Trees are only born by the month. You are either a March tree, an April tree, or a May tree. Very seldom are there any Junes, and very seldom are there any Februarys. We tree people only have offspring in the spring."

Squeaks giggled. *Giggle, Squeak, Giggle,* "Offspring in the spring! Get it?"

Abigail shook her head.

Aaron laughed. "I've never seen a bat as large as you or even been this close to a living bat before."

Squeaks puffed up her chest and stretched her wings, stretching them toward the ceiling. Slowly letting them slide down, she showed them off. She arched her back and then scratched her backside.

"Well, I have never seen a person wearing such a weird getup like yours," Abigail said in defense of Squeaks.

"I was just commenting. I didn't mean anything by it," Aaron said. "In truth, I'm glad I'm with both of you. I couldn't imagine being down here in the dark by myself. Thank you!"

The girl seemed genuinely pleased with his apology. "Shall we all be off?" Abigail shook her head back, and her hair seemed to somewhat move on its own. Aaron just looked at her.

Squeaks walked between Abigail and Aaron, flapping her wings. "We're off. This way." It was enough to distract Aaron.

The group headed farther down and deeper into the caverns. The root light started to fade. After a while, if there wasn't much of a moon, Aaron and Abigail would most likely have to hold hands and be guided by Squeaks again.

Abigail spoke more to herself than her new friends. "I hope I am with me mama and papa by me birthday in the spring. I love you. Be safe, wherever you are."

CHAPTER 7

Excitement at the Old Goat's House

"PAUL, ARE WE ALMOST THERE YET? YOU'RE bruising the insides of my legs," Miranda complained.

Paul slowed down a bit. "Sorry. I am just in a rush. I am worried about your brother."

Miranda didn't say anything.

Paul stopped after a few minutes. "Hop down, kid. I think we are about half an hour away. The walk will do you good, and you probably need to get the circulation back in your legs."

"My thighs hurt, and my butt is numb," complained Miranda. Paul chuckled, and Miranda turned and gave him a frowning look. "You had better not tell my brother, or else!"

Paul laughed. "Or else what? You will pout? Okay, enough. Just keep up. Stretch those little legs of yours. See? We are almost there. The chamber is getting wider and wider. You can hardly see the outside edges. In about ten minutes, we will go over a hill, and you will see the cottage below. Aaron's group should be coming to the cottage from the left."

"That doesn't make sense. Aaron slid down the cliff on our right," said Miranda.

"You forget that you are underground, and you are in the upper tunnel," Paul said. "They are in a lower tunnel. Their tunnel crossed underneath ours. I think they ought to be about an hour behind us."

Miranda cocked her head to the side, deep in thought. "I guess that makes sense. I haven't got my mind around some of this stuff down here. It's all new to me."

"You will figure it out," Paul said.

The two moved on. They came to the top of a hill.

"There is me cottage." Paul pointed as they made their way down the hill. "Hold up a bit. I see a light on, and there is smoke coming from the chimney. I am sure that crazy old witch is in there. Dirty rotten rat! She should be out harvesting mushrooms this time of year!"

"Paul, I have a question," asked Miranda. "Why did you and Grandpa call it the old goat's house?"

"That is an easy one," Paul said. "It used to be me cottage."

"How do you know the witch in there?"

"She used to be me witch—I mean me wife. She is me wife, the old goat that she is. Now we will wait for the others down by these rocks." Paul looked at Miranda. "Let us just sit for a few minutes."

"Why don't we just go to the cottage and wait for my brother there?" Miranda asked.

Paul ignored her for a few seconds. He realized she was looking at him and waiting for an answer. "You have a lot of questions, lassie. Some I can answer, some I cannot, and some I would rather not. When your brother gets here, then you can ask all the questions you want."

Miranda looked irritated by Paul's comment. "Why don't we just go to the cottage and wait there?" she asked again.

Paul snorted. "I would rather not. I am not sure how well I will be received."

"Why?" Miranda asked. She sat for a few more minutes, and neither spoke. Miranda stamped her right foot and stood up. "This is stupid!" she said, and before Paul could stop her, she marched down to the front door and up the porch steps and knocked. She heard a sweet little voice.

"Hold on! I'm in the middle of something!" A light came on in the room behind the door.

Miranda looked back over her shoulder and realized Paul was nowhere to be seen. She wondered whether she had made a mistake.

The door opened. A short, thin woman stood before her. She had an oven mitt on one hand and a kitchen towel hanging over her shoulder. "I'm in the middle of making my breakfast," she said, in the same accent grandma speaks in. "And who are you?"

Miranda pursed her lips for a second. "My name is Miranda. May I ask, who are you?"

"Why, I am Lily, and what brings you to my house?"

"Well, it's kind of a long story."

"That's okay; I have time. Come in, Come in, and have a seat. I don't get many visitors very often. You are quite a ways from, from? Where? Are you lost? Come in, your more than welcome, come in."

Miranda looked over her shoulder as she entered the front room. "You have no idea," she said.

"Have a seat over there, and make yourself comfortable," Lily said, pointing to a sofa with half a dozen small pillows and yarn balls. Miranda looked around the room. Lily left the front door open slightly. "Let's allow in a little fresh air. My kitchen is quite warm." The house smelled of bacon.

As Miranda made her way across the room, she looked around. There was a large picture in the center of the far wall, between two high-backed chairs. It showed a thin young girl and a handsome-looking young man in wedding clothes.

Lily giggled. "Time makes fools out of us. That was me when I was first married to my husband. I lost him quite a while ago."

Miranda sat down on the sofa just beneath the front window. To the left was a set of steps leading upstairs. To the right was the door that led to the kitchen.

Lily spoke, "Just relax. I'll go get us some tea and cookies. You look like you have been on your feet for quite some time."

"Tea sounds really good," Miranda smiled. "I'm definitely thirsty."

Lily walked back toward the kitchen. "I'll be back in a few minutes," she had picked up a tea tray that had been sitting on a stand between the chairs.

Miranda could hear Lily clanging around in the kitchen. She heard the creak of the front door.

Paul stuck his head through the crack and looked around. "I wanted to wait outside. I did not want to be in here, not just yet." He took a half dozen steps toward Miranda.

"Why?" Miranda asked.

"It is not going to end well. She is a witch."

"Yes, but you said Grandma is a witch."

"That is different. Let us go back outside," Paul pleaded. "You do not understand. This one is crazy!"

Miranda looked at the kitchen door and then back at Paul. She could hear footsteps. Before she could get up, she heard Lily.

Lily swore after she opened the kitchen door. "You! You! Yyoouuu! How dare you show up here! After everything you've done!" Lily raised her head, looked at the ceiling, took a deep breath, and then sprinted directly at Paul. The little woman was surprisingly fast. She grabbed Paul by the horn with the hand in the oven mitt, and with all her might, she started swinging the tea tray into the side of his head. "I'll finish you off!"

Bang! Clang! Bang! Clang! She showered Paul with hot tea from the little cups, which were now rolling on the floor with the cookies. Lily circled around the room. "Where's my magic wand? I'll finish you off this time!"

Miranda looked down to her right. A magic wand was beside a ball of yarn and crochet hooks. Miranda pointed at Paul, which turned Lily back around.

"You think you'll make an escape this time?" Lily screamed. She jumped forward and slammed the door shut.

Miranda bent down quickly, snatched up the wand, and shoved it down behind the cushions on the sofa.

The witch pushed Paul over toward the stairs. She kicked the front door. She kicked Paul. She kicked the chairs. Miranda started to think the woman was crazy. *She's going to kill us both*, Miranda thought. "Lily, what do you mean by wand?" Miranda shouted.

"My magic wand! I always forget where I lay it!" Lily answered.

I need to keep talking to Lily, Miranda thought. "He told me this was a safe place to come."

"For you, yes. For him, no!" Lily replied.

"Grandpa said Paul and I would be safe here!" Miranda shouted.

"Who's Grandpa?" Lily asked.

"He told Paul to bring me and my brother here."

"Who is your grandpa?"

"Grandpa Eddie. Edward Meyer."

Lily stopped for a minute. She looked at the ceiling and shook her head in confusion. "Emma and Eddie disappeared. That doesn't make any sense."

Paul trotted over and sat between the two chairs. Lily scowled at him. Miranda sat back on the sofa, making sure she was sitting on the cushion concealing the wand. She could hear kids coming up the walkway and giggling. Aaron was laughing and giggling with his new friends.

"That's my brother!" Miranda jumped up, ran over, and opened the front door. "In here! Hurry, In here, We're all in here!"

Lily walked over and picked up the tea tray. "I'm going to get my breakfast before it burns. Maybe I'll get lucky and find my wand. I probably left it in the kitchen," she mumbled, going into the kitchen.

Paul looked at Miranda, and Miranda looked at Paul. Abigail, Aaron, and Squeaks slid in through the front door. They all stood in a huddle. Miranda hugged Aaron as if she had not seen him for a year. Lily walked back into the living room. She put one hand over her heart and pointed at the twins with the other. She then passed out. All the kids rushed forward and helped her to one of the chairs. It took a couple of minutes for her to come around.

Lily looked at Aaron and then looked at Miranda again. "Twins?"

Paul jumped up. As heavy as he was, the cottage shook. "Mallacht! (Cursed)," He stomped his foot. "Twins! Identical twins! Just like I told you! Look at me. Just look what you did to me! Nobody can fix me. Not even you."

Lily started to cry, rocking back and forth, almost in shock.

"Look at your banjaxed piece-of-crap husband! The one who was supposedly whoring around on you, out on a tear!" Paul shouted. "Did you think for one second that I might have been telling you the truth! The rock-solid honest truth! I spent me months dragging these twins across the World Under just to get them to a safe place on the surface. I finally made it home, knackered and tired, only to have me wife accuse me of cheating and turn me into a goat! And you did not even do that right! Thank goodness I can still speak. I ran for me life! Fireballs flying everywhere! Turned into a goat, with half me fur missing from me hindquarters—the thanks I get!"

Lily was now sobbing.

Paul continued. "Ruined our marriage. Threw half our lives away. All you had to do was believe me! We could have gone to the surface; you could have seen the twins there. You are one crazy woman!"

At that point, Miranda had had enough. She jumped up and slapped Paul across the side of his face. "Stop! Just look at her!"

Paul looked at Lily, who was shaking and crying. "Look at her? Look at me! I am a bloody goat!" He turned around and flopped back down in front of the fireplace. The cottage shook again. "I cannot even sit in me own manky chair," he muttered.

At that point, Miranda sidled up to Abigail and Squeaks, and without words, the girls took Lily into the kitchen. Paul sat there on the floor, muttering under his breath, looking out the front door.

Aaron smiled at Paul. "Well, nobody's dead yet!"

CHAPTER 8

A Birthday to Remember

"I T'S MY BIRTHDAY. I'M GOING TO JOIN SISSY." Aaron went to the kitchen to be with Miranda. The girls had spent some time talking with Lily. Lily seemed to snap back to herself. She seemed surprised by all the commotion in the cottage but also happy at finding out it was the twins' birthday. She was enjoying the company now. She had all the kids work with her to make a ton of apple tarts. Lily said they were Paul's favorite snack. She used to always keep some ready for Paul when he returned on leave. After the apple tarts were in the oven, the group started to make birthday cookies in true World Under fashion.

After a loud morning, everyone sat down in the living room, enjoying raspberry tea and apple tarts. When Lily heard the bell on the stove go off, she got up and went back into the kitchen to get the birthday cookies. Apparently, down here, people did not receive cake for their birthdays. They received sugar cookies made by friends. Most people would decorate them however they wanted. Aaron made Miranda a huge smiley-face cookie. Miranda made Aaron a large crocodile head. Squeaks and Abigail also enjoyed making birthday cookies. Squeaks made an Aaron and a Miranda gingerbread-looking sugar cookie and decorated them just like the twins. Abigail made a sugar cookie for Miranda like the one Squeaks had made. She gave the Miranda-looking cookie a little crown on her head. For Aaron, she made a sugar cookie of herself on one side of Aaron and Squeaks on the other. Miranda stared at the cookie for a few minutes, and then she looked at Abigail and said, "That's nice." She kind of pursed her lips but didn't say anything else.

Abigail gave her half a smile. "Thank you."

Aaron seemed oblivious to the exchange.

Lily had made a couple of cookies for Paul as well. He seemed to enjoy them. Lily got up and said, "While you guys are relaxing, I'm going to go clean up some of the mess and start preparing dinner since we have so many guests here." She headed back into the kitchen. It almost seemed as if she just wanted to be alone.

After a while, Lily reentered the living room as they were all just lying around. The kids were teasing Paul with goat noises. Paul did not seem to mind. Miranda got up from the sofa, grabbed a couple more apple tarts, and then sat down on the floor by Paul. She leaned against his thick fur and fed him more tarts. Lily quietly watched the exchange between Paul and Miranda.

Lily studied all the kids. She took in the whole scene. She smiled, walked over and picked up a couple more apple tarts from the bent tea tray, and handed them to Miranda. Then she went over and sat down in her favorite chair, picked up her crochet hooks, and began to crochet on an afghan she had been working on for quite some time. The group started explaining who they were and where they had come from. They also shared the activities they liked and didn't like. Abigail seemed shy at first. Squeaks seemed to want to take center stage. They talked all through their dinner. Lily explained who she was. She talked about what it was like to grow up in a witch tribe. They learned more about Abigail's banishment and the task of locating her parents. Late that evening, when everyone looked very tired, Paul directed the kids to get their teeth brushed, and Lily suggested the girls join her upstairs in their old bedroom. Aaron brushed Paul's teeth again. Paul took a spot near the fireplace, facing the front door. Aaron took the sofa. It had been one of the busiest days of their lives. There would be many more to follow. After Paul was sure Aaron was asleep and snoring away, he got up, went over, and lay against the front door.

Lily came downstairs the next morning and said, "I lost something."

Paul lifted his head. "No, Miranda came downstairs last night. She is lying at the opposite end of the sofa from her brother."

"No," Lily said. "I lost my husband, and I'm very sorry."

Paul just looked at Lily. He rose and moved across the room. He stood on his back legs, put his front legs on her shoulders, and looked deep into her eyes. "You have not lost anything. I forgave you the day you did this to me. The very hour I ran from this house. I love you Lily, and I always will." He shook his head, dropped down, trotted over to the fire, and lay back down.

"Paul, you know you are me best friend. I've missed you all these years," Lily said.

"Crazy woman," Paul retorted.

Lily gave a half smile. "I guess I'd better get into the kitchen and start whipping up some breakfast for all these bellies." She scooted into the kitchen.

Within an hour, all the girls were downstairs and making a lot of noise. Paul pretended it bothered him, but in truth, it was heavenly. The commotion was unreal. When they were all seated at the table, Paul addressed the group. "Lily and I decided while talking early this morning that we would wait here another day or two to find out how Grandma is doing. That would be the safest course of action. If we do not hear anything within two days, possibly three at the most, Lily will go to the surface and try to find out herself."

Miranda and Aaron looked concerned. Lily then spoke up. "Since none of us know what the International World Under Senate is doing other than the rumors I heard last spring, the only way we can safely find out what's happening to all the trees is to approach the Council of Witches. We will also inform them of what has happened to Abigail. If the rumors I heard a couple of years ago are true, the governing bodies are rounding up the trees for work details. It will be extremely difficult to find out where Abigail's parents were sent. It would also be extremely dangerous for Abigail to be out alone looking for her parents. I don't get out and socialize very much. Therefore, Abigail, we want you to stay with us. We will all look for your parents as we take Aaron and Miranda across the World Under to the Council of Witches. This will give us the opportunity to find out if this is something only occurring in our cavern or worse."

Paul interrupted. "This is the safest place for all three of you. Squeaks, since you do not need a legal guardian, you can decide to do whatever you want. That being said, you are welcome to stay with the group."

Squeak, Squeak, "Me mates." Squeaks hugged Abigail.

Paul nodded. "That settles it."

"Hopefully we know something within the next day or two about Grandma, and then we will set out for the Council of Witches," Lily said.

Nobody had any questions since the twins were new to the World Under and didn't understand it.

"I guess our business is finished for now," Lily said. "Shall the kids go out and play a game? I think there's a bucket with a lid around here somewhere that would work well as a flying disc."

The group cleared the table and washed the dishes. They then headed out the front door. They played with the lid like a regular flying disc but then developed some new games since they had such a skilled adversary in Squeaks.

The next two days continued to go pretty much like the first. On the second day, when Lily's grand-father clock chimed two o'clock just as the glow of the main root was at its brightest, everyone headed inside for lunch. They had all been playing a game with a soccer ball that Lily had ran across when cleaning out her shed. Miranda, Aaron, and Abigail would hold hands in a circle. Squeaks would drop a ball Lily had found down through the center of the circle and then fly around the outside of the circle at lightning speed. The group would watch the ball fall. The one closest to where the ball was about to land would yell out, "Marco!" Squeaks would have to make it the rest of the way around the circle, zoom underneath their legs, and snatch the ball before it landed on the ground. She would then scream, "Polo!" and take the ball up to the cavern ceiling before dropping it again.

Lunch was tomato soup with grilled cheese sandwiches. Lily said something simple would be good. The pantry was becoming bare. Lily set the plate of sandwiches in front of Aaron. Aaron, who typically lost out to his sister, made his move. He snatched two sandwiches off the top of the stack. Each sandwich had a long toothpick sticking out of the top. "For once, I'm not getting the leftovers," he said.

The girls looked at one another. The plate made it around the table. All the girls' eyes were on Aaron as he took bites out of both sandwiches, holding one in each hand.

Lily walked back into the room. She looked at Aaron and looked at the toothpicks on his plate. "How is everything?" she asked.

With loaded cheeks, Aaron said, "Best grilled cheese I ever had. What were those crunchy things?"

Miranda grinned. "Well, Brother, you know how I like to burst your bubble?"

"Yeah??" said Aaron suspiciously.

Miranda's grin widened. "Those sandwiches had been made special for Squeaks! Remember the crickets that we all collected out by the fence yesterday! Those were the crunchy things."

Aaron's eyes got big. He put a hand over his mouth and made a gagging sound. *Gaa gha uugh ga!* He flipped his chair over and ran up the steps.

Paul yelled after him, "Watch it! And clean up any mess you make!" The girls were roaring with laughter. Paul muttered, "For once, he will get the bathroom first too."

Just then, there was a knock at the front door. Lily got up and went quickly to answer it. She peeked through the little window. It was Grandpa. She threw open the door, and Eddie walked in. He dropped his bag not far from the sofa and said, "I can't stay long. I just had to let you know what was going on."

Aaron, who had made it halfway back down the stairs, stared over the railing. All the girls left their lunch in the dining room. Grandpa addressed the group.

"Grandma's not doing well. She's been unconscious ever since the accident. I think the doctors are keeping her that way, but they won't tell me much. I figured it would be better for Lily to take a shot at it. Grandma may have had a stroke. I needed to talk to you two anyhow," he said, addressing the twins. He pulled out two small birthday gifts.

The twins looked at them. Miranda looked as if she were about to cry. Aaron looked mad.

"I'll get my things," Lily said, and she quietly headed upstairs.

Grandpa knelt between the twins. Aaron had come all the way downstairs and was standing next to Miranda. Grandpa said, "I'm sure by now you have figured some of this stuff out, like the fact that we are not your grandparents. You are the last two members of the royal family, the Dunkeld line, and we are not royalty."

"That says it all!" Aaron shouted.

Miranda jumped forward and hugged Grandpa. "Is Grandma going to be okay?" she asked.

"I don't know Miranda. Lily has a better shot at healing grandma than any of those quacks up there."

Lily came back down the stairs. She had two bags. She walked over, picked up Grandpa's bag, and headed for the kitchen to gather food and water for the trip.

Just then, Aaron spoke up. "Why would you lie to us?"

"Easy," Paul said.

Grandpa looked at Aaron with a sad helpless expression. Miranda backed away. Aaron threw down his gift and bolted out the door.

Lily intervened. "We need to go, Eddie."

Abigail and Squeaks came to stand by Miranda. They didn't say anything; they just put their arms around her.

"In the morning, we will head to the Council of Witches. We have got a long journey ahead of us. Edward, Lily, be safe," Paul said.

"Because of time," Lily pointed out. "We are going to take the coach. I would leave it for you, but I think we need it more. You'll have to walk." She had an old wooden coach with a one-cylinder engine that had to be started with a rope. It made a heck of a racket but was a lot faster than walking.

"Well, I'd better go get Aaron," Paul said, shaking his head.

Miranda stated, "No, he needs me."

Paul looked at her. "Take Squeaks as well. Squeaks can see people way off in the distance." Squeaks nodded, and Miranda and Squeaks walked out the door.

Within a minute, Grandpa and Lily went out the back door, which gave Paul some time to talk to Abigail. Abigail didn't say anything; she just listened.

"We are going to head to the Council of Witches. And see if we can find a safe place for the twins during our trip across the World Under. As we go, we will also try to find out what is going on with the evergreen deciduous clans. It is very important that I get the twins to the Council of Witches. They are the last of the royal bloodline. I have sworn an oath to protect the royal family, and I would give me life trying. I love them as if they were me own. There are hundreds, if not thousands, of witches and wizards down here who would be just as happy to see the twins dead. I do not know what the outcome of the council is going to be, but I think it is the best viable option since witches and the New Croatoan Order do not get along. Obviously, since we have been attacked on the surface, there must be a group who know of the twin's existence. The worst part is, I do not even know which group is after us. Other than the two Croatoan druids who tried to kill us, me best guess is that it has to do with the international lawmakers at the Senate. I repeat this trip will also help us find out what is going on with your people. Keep all this under your hat, especially if we encounter strangers. Stick with me, lassie," Paul explained.

Abigail slowly nodded.

"Thank you, Abigail," Paul said as he bowed his head toward her. "We will get your situation straightened out as well. I promise, and that is not just me words. It is me word."

CHAPTER 9

Miranda's Wise Counsel

IRANDA AND SQUEAKS CAUGHT UP TO AARON, who had run toward the center of the large cavern. He was kneeling at the edge of a field of mushrooms as large as cars. Miranda told Squeaks to go back to the cottage to tell Paul she had found her brother. Squeaks shook her head.

Miranda gave her a funny look. "Why not?"

Squeaks flew over and picked up a rock. Next, she flew over the field of mushrooms and dropped the rock. A large mushroom about twenty feet away stretched up its tongue and snatched the rock out of the air.

Squeaks came back to Miranda. *Squeak, Squeak,* "Yellow mushrooms good. Red mushrooms bad. Brown mushrooms bad." Aaron was leaning on the top of a yellow mushroom. "Okay, I'll go back to the cottage." Off Squeaks went.

"Aaron, I'm as worried as you are," Miranda said.

Aaron shook his head. "No, I've been so stupid. I didn't realize they weren't our grandparents. I'm supposed to be smarter than most people."

Miranda sat down and put her arm around him. "You are smarter than most people in some ways, maybe even most ways. You can see how things work and what they can be good for. But sometimes you can be so smart that you are dumb."

Aaron looked up at her.

"I heard the Sabatini's talking, and then Paul told Squeaks we were royalty," Miranda said.

"Yeah, I didn't get it, though. I just thought we were special," Aaron replied.

"We had just been attacked!" Miranda responded. "We had just been informed of the World Under. We were running for our lives. We were being led by a talking goat! There were lots of things we didn't get. And now there's this," she said, pointing toward the mushrooms. "There is a whole world we know nothing about—talking bats, tree people, witches, and wizards, not to mention mushrooms that can eat us. The Croatoan Druids want us dead!"

Aaron took a deep breath. "At least I have you."

"Aaron, you also have Grandma and Grandpa. They may not be ours by blood, but they love us very much. You can't be mad because they lied to us. I don't like being lied to either. Everything that was done was done to keep us safe and alive. I may not like it, but I can see how it was. I might even kick that stupid goat in the shin for you if you want."

"I agree," Aaron said.

"One more thing, Aaron. When you slipped down that cliff of rocks, Paul went nuts. He was getting ready to take me and jump off that cliff to go after you. The scary thing is, I would have gone with him. I can see now that Paul has been silently watching out for us our entire lives. I can also see that he would do just about anything for us. Let's go back to the cottage and try to figure out what's going on and to help Abigail. I can tell you like her. Not sure why—she is kinda gangly and not very pretty."

"Shut up!" Aaron said as he stood up and headed back toward the cottage.

"I see you blushing," teased Miranda as she took off running.

When they got back to the cottage, no one said much to the twins. True to her word, Miranda went up to Paul and kicked him in the shin. "Ouch! What gives?" Paul asked.

"No more lies," replied Miranda as she continued into the kitchen.

Aaron slumped on the sofa. The other girls followed Miranda. Paul flopped down in front of the fire. "You, okay?" Paul asked.

"Yup," Aaron replied.

Paul lowered his head back onto his knee. He licked his shin. "I would rather take a kick to the shin than eat a cricket sandwich," he teased, and Aaron smiled. "Tomorrow is going to be another big day," Paul said.

He got up and went to the kitchen to tell the girls what needed to be done.

The group made an early night of it. All the girls headed upstairs. Paul walked over to his chair, grabbed a pillow with his mouth, and put it on the side of the sofa opposite Aaron. "That is for your other moody lassie, Your Majesty." He then went to the front door and lay down with his back against it.

CHAPTER 10

A New Journey in a Better Direction

THE GROUP GOT UP EARLY. SURE ENOUGH, MIRANDA was on the opposite end of the sofa. Abigail and Squeaks woke Paul. Everyone started packing. They pretty much emptied the pantry. "At least on this trip, we won't go hungry," Aaron said.

The kids filled Paul's saddlebags. Paul walked around the house and watched all the kids go out the front door. "Goodbye, me old house. It does not seem like I get to see much of you." Paul walked out the front door, leaving it open.

The group headed down toward the mushroom patch, turned left, and headed northeast. "Red mushrooms and brown mushrooms you stay away from. The red ones will grab you and eat you, and the brown ones use spores and long vines at their base. They will put you to sleep with a cloud of spores and then pull you in and eat you," Paul told them.

They noticed that the World Under changed the deeper they went. It turned into fields of green clovers with tall blue grassy patches. There were also bushes and shrubs. No more was it just brown dirt and rocky wall caverns. As they headed down, the roots spread out across the ceiling of the chamber, instead of one or two in the center. It looked as if someone had painted branches from one end of the cavern to the other. It was a beautiful and amazing place.

Aaron spoke up. "To think nobody on the surface knows this is here."

Paul looked at Aaron. "Some do. Look at the Sabatini family," he pointed out.

Miranda looked at Paul, "Yeah, but they had to destroy their business."

Paul shook his head, "Please. Do you think they are not just going to build a new one? They know what is important. Life is about family, or at least about those who care for each other."

Squeaks looked at Abigail and squeaked.

The group continued on. They walked among towering stalactites and stalagmites that supported the massive cavern ceiling. The grass didn't grow only on the ground; there were mosses that grew on the walls as well. They were not just green; there were all shades of yellow and orange and even some blues. A swarm of glowing butterflies flew in front of the group.

"This place is truly amazing!" Miranda said.

Paul told the group, "Let's keep moving. We have a place to go, a place to be, and a place to leave behind."

Aaron giggled.

"So, we are back to ourselves," Paul added. "The brain gears click back into place."

"Yep," Aaron said.

Miranda and Aaron were passing the magic wand back and forth. Neither was having much luck with it. Aaron was only able to produce small wisps of smoke but nothing more. Miranda, however, was able to get a small flame going at the tip of the wand.

After a half hour, Paul interrupted. "I want to try something. Miranda, hand me magic wand to Abigail." Paul was watching Abigail watch the twins.

Abigail took the wand. The group stopped walking.

"Abigail," Paul directed. "Point the wand at that rock over there."

Abigail did as Paul advised. Something interesting was happening. It was as if the magic wand had a mind of its own, as if it were a living thing. It started to wriggle around in Abigail's hand as if it were alive.

"Point at the rock again," Paul said. "Say the word for *fire*: *tine*."

Fire did not come from the wand. The rock started to lift up into the air and then split in half and fell to the ground. Paul requested; she try it again. The two halves flew one hundred feet away, as if Abigail had thrown them.

"That I did not expect," Paul said. "I think we are all in agreement that once we get into town, Abigail keeps me wand. She seems to have the most ability to fend off an attack. Let us do it one more time, Abigail. This time, I want you to say, 'Tilgeadh.' The word *tilgeadh* means *throw*."

Abigail did as Paul said. This time, she threw the rock two hundred feet. Everyone was amazed. Paul pointed his nose, "Abigail see that small pebble by me foot?"

She did it again. The rock hit Paul right between the horns. He dropped to the ground. Everyone rushed toward Paul. As they got to him, he jumped up. "Perfect! Let us not do that again, but it was perfect. I want you to walk about twenty feet in front of the group. Keep practicing. Throw rocks at any red or brown mushrooms you see. Work on your aim."

Abigail did as he said.

Paul told the twins, "I think this is best. She will be able to protect herself. She even has control over it. She seems to be a natural. With her ahead of us, I can talk to you both."

Paul began again, "When I left ten years ago, The World Under international community was upset with the trees. The trees, the redwood clans out west, had been protecting and hiding gargoyles. There were not many gargoyles left, because for about two hundred years, they had been imprisoned and used as slaves. If me hunch is correct—and me hunches almost always are—the international community has chosen a new workforce. She is in even more danger than the two of you. They must be replacing the gargoyles with the trees. Abigail's being with us is probably the safest place for her now. She is under our protection, not that there is much of it. Half the world would be upset to find out there is still royalty left alive. They would want you dead."

"Now that we're alone," Miranda interrupted. "I have a question for you, Brother. Ignore the goat. What's up with you liking Abigail?"

Aaron didn't say anything for a long time.

"Come on now. We have no secrets. I'm always honest with you, even if you don't like it."

Paul backed off a little bit, giving the twins a little distance.

"I don't know. I look at her face, and my stomach gets all jittery," Aaron replied.

"Come on," huffed Miranda.

Aaron looked sideways at his sister. "I don't care what you think. I think she's gorgeous."

Miranda opened her mouth, closed it, then opened it again, but Paul interrupted. "Aaron, your odds are not good. She carries a lot of baggage."

Miranda said, "Thank you Mr. Nosy Goat."

"Suit yourself. She is going to break your heart," Paul replied.

Paul cleared his throat. "One more thing for you two knuckle heads to understand down in our world. Oh, Squeaks, did you get all that?"

Squeaks was up ahead. She had hitched a ride with Abigail, wrapping her wings around Abigail's shoulders piggyback-style.

Paul said, "So the numbskulls understand you can hear everything within a quarter mile. Squeaks, please do not repeat what they have just discussed. Let the lad make a fool out of himself on his own. I do not think he needs our assistance on this subject."

Squeaks turned, looked at the three of them, and nodded.

"Thanks, lassie," replied Paul, and Squeaks turned her head back in a forward direction. "In about an hour or so, we are going to come upon a town," Paul added.

As they got closer to the town, passing farms along the way, Paul realized there was a problem. "Everybody hold up a minute," he said.

They all huddled around Paul. Abigail was still holding the magic wand.

"I want you to hide me magic wand in your hair or someplace where you can get to it quickly and easily, Abigail. The villagers may have a problem if a tree is walking around carrying a magic wand."

Abigail held the magic wand in front of her. It started to wiggle in her hand, as it had earlier. She pointed it toward her waist. Paul's magic wand lengthened and followed her belt loops all the way around her kilt.

"That's impressive," Miranda stated.

"Thank you," Abigail replied. "It is almost like an extension of me arm."

"That makes sense," Aaron said. "You are part tree."

"Okay, is everybody paying attention?" Paul asked. "Our main problem is that we are all in one group.

Two kids, a bat, a goat, and a deciduous tree girl walk into a town."

Giggle, Squeak, Squeak, "Sounds like the start of a joke," said Squeaks, giggling.

"Knock it off," Paul said. "That is a major problem. There are no adults with us. We are fine here. We will probably be fine in this town, but when we get to the city, there are going to be problems. We must find someone in this town or the next with a ship who is willing to take us from Boston to the witches' tribal lands. It will be a lot more work than you realize."

"Not to mention a talking goat," Aaron quipped.

"I can explain being a goat by the fact that I am a wizard. Another question: Who here has money?"

Abigail spoke up. "Lily gave me a little purse with money when she left with your grandpa. I put it in me belt pouch."

"We will count it when we get to a safe quiet place in town," Paul said. "We need to see if there are any soldiers or guardsmen. Squeaks, can you fly around the outside of the town? Then you can tell me what you see and hear with those beautifully nosy ears you have."

Squeaks took off. The twins looked at each other. "It's amazing how fast she is," Miranda said. She also pointed out that Lily had packed extra clothes in all their school backpacks. Miranda had received a couple of Lily's outfits. Everyone had been given a coat or a jacket. Aaron and Abigail each had received one of Paul's old coats. Aaron's was an old brown leather coat and was a bit large for him. He also had received a couple of T-shirts. Abigail's coat was one of Paul's old navy trench coats. It had a large hood that could hide most of her head from view. They would not look as out of place in their jeans and trainers.

Paul looked at Miranda and Aaron, trying to decide which twin looked older. Everyone had pulled out and put on their coats. Since neither of the twins looked old enough, Paul said, "Miranda, you ride on me back; it will make you look taller. You will look more ladylike." He directed Aaron to walk beside Abigail, behind Miranda and himself. Aaron smiled. Abigail ignored him.

As they walked past a group of farmers out in the field, one of the farmers yelled, "Hey, is that goat for sale?"

Miranda shook her head no.

"Really?" Paul muttered. To Miranda, he said under his breath toward the farmers, "Be nice now, or I will be burning your britches!"

"You said we need money," Miranda teased.

"Do you not know why they want to buy me?" Paul asked.

"No," answered Miranda.

"Goats, sheep, and pigs are the main sources of meat in the World Under. We do not have many cows. Shorter daylight means shorter grasses. Cows need big, tall grasses and lots of daylight. You are riding on the steak of the World Under. I prefer not to be sold," Paul stated.

Squeaks returned to the group. "It looks like a little town no different from any other," she said.

As the group walked into the little town, they passed an old farmer who had the duty of being the town watchman. He nodded toward them as if to say, "You may pass." Then he spoke. "Welcome to Georgetown."

Miranda slid off Paul's back once they were inside the little town. They passed half a dozen houses with little courtyards that had chickens running around in them. They passed a bank and then a courthouse. There was a cemetery between the courthouse and a tiny church. There were a couple of shops across the road, including a bakery. They could smell the bread. The town had a hardware store and next to it a magic shop named, The Appalachian All American Magic Supplies and Comics, with a sign below that read, "Comics and Candies. Sweets for All." Next, there was a bar beside a women's clothing shop.

Abigail and Squeaks were giggling. Aaron wanted to know what was so funny. Paul responded, "If you do not know, then I am not telling you."

Miranda leaned over and whispered in Aaron's ear. Aaron turned bright pink.

It was a nice little town. They passed a few more houses, which had a look of fine craftsmanship to them.

They came upon a corner bistro called Ollie's Pasta and Pies. The bistro had a sign saying there was a room for rent. "Everyone wait here," Paul said. Paul took Miranda inside with him.

In a few minutes, a short, chubby Italian man with a handlebar mustache came outside. He was wearing a red-and-white striped apron. "I'm Ollie. Welcome, wizard and all. Business is business. Welcome. No mutton or chevon tonight." There were about six people sitting up toward the bar and another couple over in a cozy corner booth near the front window.

The group were ushered to a long table, where they all sat, except for Paul, who stood at the end and looked irritated at Ollie's question of "Are you housebroken?"

"I told you! I am a wizard!"

"You might be a wizard, but your back end doesn't look like one," the owner said waggling his finger and chuckling. The entire group burst out laughing, and the owner shook his head.

One of the guys sitting at the bar came over to them and sat down. "Hello. My name is Jack," he said. "I overheard something about a talking wizard that is a goat. I am being nosy now, not that I have ever been shy! What brings you to this quiet little town?" Jack then turned to the owner, "Oliver, can you please get this group some pizza pies?"

Squeaks nodded. "With anchovies!"

"Okay, anchovies on one." Aaron decided to be careful about what he ate from there on out.

"The girl and the goat talked to Ollie about a room and a boat when they first came in. I always jump on a business deal when I see an opportunity," Jack stated. "I just happen to own a little boat. You see, I'm a river runner. Move items from here to there in my free time. I make two trips a year around the World Under."

"We may not have much money," Paul said. "Abigail, let us see what Lily has gifted us to work within that small purse of hers. Open it, lassie, and let's see what the nuts add up to."

Abigail poured the contents of the purse onto the table in front of Miranda, who was sitting across the table. Paul walked over beside Miranda. Jack's eyes were huge.

Paul listed aloud, "two copper penny, six copper bit, twelve copper shillien, three copper jillien, seven gold rainbow, one silver rainbow, two gold star, more than two dozen silver stars, and a small green gem." Finishing with a long whistle.

Paul stated. "That crazy witch of mine must have saved every copper and silver she made while harvesting and selling mushroom spores in the last nine years. She never did waste anything. Paul laughed to himself. It is very tricky to harvest the red ones; she would always stand behind a full-body dressing mirror as she harvested spores." Paul chuckled to himself. *That is me witch.*

Jack looked at Paul. "Wow, a dozen silver stars alone are worth three to four years' income to most. And I couldn't tell you what the green gem is worth."

Paul looked at Jack. "How much to move our merchandise across the World Under?"

Jack didn't hesitate. "Three silver stars."

Paul interrupted. "Twelve stars then. The cargo is quite valuable to me."

For the first time, Jack hesitated. "I have to go all the way around to London," he said.

"So, you will be able to stop in Berlin on the way?" Paul asked.

Jack responded, "It's a little houseboat, not a cargo freighter! I'm actually a member of the London navy, and I wouldn't want to get in any trouble. We used to be part of the royal navy, until the royals were all eliminated. Each cavern state took a portion of the ships. Still, I guess things haven't really changed much."

"Thank you very much for your hospitality. How long until we can get underway?" Paul asked.

"I haven't agreed to any deal yet," Jack said. "Maybe a day, if you don't mind hanging around for a day or so."

Oliver came out with the pizzas and set them all around the table. "You's getting along with my future son-in-law here?"

"I think we have a job for him," Paul told Oliver.

Jack nodded. "Done. Oliver, have Suzanne come out here, please."

Oliver went back to the kitchen and soon reappeared with a curvy young woman. She had black hair, green eyes, and rosy cheeks. She wore a long sundress with a red-and-white striped apron over it. Jack introduced her to Paul. "Not too often do you get to meet a talking goat," Jack joked.

"Well," Paul said, "I am really a wizard, not a goat."

Jack explained to Suzanne that he would be leaving two days earlier than planned. She seemed to lose a little of her happiness, until Jack reached for the money and handed her eight of the twelve silver stars. "You can get started on having our house built while I am away. It's like getting two to three years' worth of wages in a month," he said. "Also, have Bones make four extra barrels for my next trip."

"Shhh!" said Suzanne.

"So, the real question is, what am I smuggling?" Jack asked.

Oliver, looking down at the money, interrupted. "Wait a minute." He addressed the people at the bar and the couple in the corner booth. "Can I have your attention, please? I'm closing the restaurant early tonight." There were some whispers and muttering, but no one seemed overly upset. "If fact, what drinks and dinner you've had are on the house. Don't worry about the tab."

The men at the bar cheered. That seemed to change everyone's mood. Within a few minutes, the restaurant was empty. The front door was closed and locked.

Jack said, "There've been a lot of funny rumors of changes to the government."

"Our senator died," said Suzanne.

Oliver interrupted. "Likely killed!"

Abigail gave Oliver a copper jillien for the room, which he pocketed. "Your group has the use of the upstairs for the night," Oliver said. "There are two rooms and a small kitchenette."

"So, what are we smuggling?" Jack asked again.

"Apparently, you are not going to be deterred," Paul stated.

Abigail, who was always quiet, spoke up. "Us." She pointed across the table at Miranda and at Aaron.

"Okay, if you don't feel like telling me, I guess you don't have to," Jack responded.

Miranda spoke before Paul could say anything. "I've had enough of fibs and lies. Before Paul lies to you and he will, I will tell you the truth. My name is Miranda, and this is my brother, Aaron. We are the royal twins. We were smuggled out of the World Under ten years ago. So, I guess we are your precious cargo."

Jack, Oliver, and Suzanne just looked at them. Suzanne spoke with an Italian accent. "That is so ridiculous I guess it must be true." She had a seat with the group and ate a slice of pie.

The group continued eating and making jokes. The travelers were eventually ushered upstairs. After they were in the room, Paul asked, "Why did you choose to tell them?"

Miranda smiled. "They answered the question for me—at least Jack did. I don't know how much money is worth here, but he seemed very honest and very fair. He could have asked for a lot more, and he accepted more than a fair price. I figure we can't go around not trusting anybody. Eventually, you have to pick and choose who you can trust and who you can't."

Paul shook his head. "Sometimes I wonder if you are the smart one."

Aaron head whipped around. "Ouch. That hurts."

"Okay, I want everyone on guard because we do not really know them yet. Tomorrow is another day, and I have a feeling it will be another long one," Paul said.

CHAPTER 11

Long Walk off a Short Dock

THE GROUP GOT UP EARLY THE NEXT MORNING. IT DID not take long to get ready to leave. Oliver invited them down to enjoy breakfast with Suzanne and himself. Suzanne made blueberry pancakes. There seemed to be an endless supply of them.

Jack entered in through the front door just as the group were finishing breakfast. Suzanne rushed over to Jack and gave him a big hug and a long kiss.

"I see everyone is up and busy." Oliver interrupted. "It was a pleasure to meet both of you. I hope someday you will return." He gave Miranda and Aaron a small bow. "I've got to get ready for a long day. Saturdays are always busy around here."

Aaron spoke up. "It's been a week since the accident. Somehow, I've lost all track of time."

Jack came over and sat down at the table. Suzanne gave him a tall stack of pancakes. "Thank you, my love," he said. "We are a full day's walk to Boston. I've decided not to walk. I have hired a coach. It should be here around eight o'clock. It's the least I can do since you paid me so handsomely. I think we've got about half an hour before it gets here. There's no rush, as he has been paid for the whole day."

Suzanne dabbed her eyes with a handkerchief and went back into the kitchen.

"They seem like really good people." Paul said.

"They are," Jack said. "I'm going to miss her. The last time I told her I would be gone for six months, it turned into twelve. We had to wait on two ships that were transporting trees from Appalachia to Queensland. It caused all incoming and outgoing watercraft permits to be delayed."

Wham! If a look could kill. Abigail was staring Jack down, eye to eye. She had stood up and leaned over the table scattering plates, silverware and glasses. At the same time, she grabbed Jack by the collar with one hand and was pulling her sheath knife from her belt, with the other. She pressed her nose up against Jacks nose. "Where are me parents?" she demanded.

Jack slowly pulled away. Paul literally jumped up onto the table. "That was a year ago, Abigail, not a month," Paul shouted. He had wedged himself between the both of them. Miranda and Aaron each grabbed one of Abigail's arms.

Jack said, "I'm not sure what you are talking about. The chancellor and the Senate passed a law about seven years ago requiring all trees to report to work camps. This last year, a small group of Senate Guard started rounding up the leftovers. I just assumed you belonged to Paul or the royal twins." The news did not bode well for Abigail.

"Abigail, sit down," Paul commanded. "We are guests here."

Abigail gritted her teeth and slowly sat down. The twins looked at each other, wondering what was going to happen next. Paul explained Abigail's situation to Jack: her parents had been taken, and the group were looking to find them. Jack apologized, but it didn't seem to make a lot of difference to Abigail. She seemed to take the line of thought "If you don't oppose it, you obviously support it."

Just then, the coach arrived out front—perfect timing. The group were ushered out the front door with all their bags, including a couple Jack had set on the front stoop. The coach looked to be from the 1800s, the kind one saw in New York pulled by a team of horses. Except it didn't have a team of horses.

"This is Mayor George Somerson's personal coach," Jack said, acting as if there were no problems. The coach was driven by a tall, strong man who wore a black suit with a top hat. Everything matched. The twins didn't notice any of that, however; they were staring at a pair of enormous spiders the size of a rhinoceros. They were huge, muscular, hairy spiders. One was brown-ish black, and the other was all black.

The coachman opened the door and invited every-one to get in. Abigail took a seat in the far corner, as far away from Jack as she could get. The coachman loaded the bags into the back. Squeaks flew up and sat on the roof behind the coachman. Jack addressed Paul. "We should be there in about three to four hours. Much bet-ter than a full day of aching feet and legs."

"Thank you very much, Jack," Paul said.

Within minutes, the group had left the little town behind. Everyone was busy looking out the windows at the amazing place. Who would have ever thought of a spider-drawn carriage? It was a bumpy ride.

Paul finally addressed Abigail. "We will get this straightened out as soon as I take care of Miranda and Aaron's safety. I will spend the rest of me life making things right for you, young lassie."

Jack said, "I am truly sorry I did not understand. I wasn't part of the process that has been taking place down here. Never have I once been involved with the moving of people."

Abigail had a defeated look on her face. Aaron was stuck sitting between his sister and Abigail. He didn't know what to say to her. He just reached over and put his hand over hers. Abigail didn't pull away. Instead, she wrapped her index finger over his. That seemed to irritate Miranda. Abigail ignored Jack and kept staring out the window.

It did not take long for the coach to make the trip. Paul requested that the coach stop. "Let us walk from here."

Everybody got out of the coach. Paul whispered into Squeaks' ear. She took to the air. Everyone looked up and noticed hundreds of bats flying around. Some were leaving the city, and some were coming in. The city was sprawled out in front of them. It went from one side of the cavern to the other as far as the eye could see. Boston was magnificent. It wasn't small. It might have been as large as New York City. They could barely see an ocean on the opposite side. There was a small group of travelers heading away from the city on foot.

Jack stopped Paul. Jack talked to the group passing by. Aaron, Miranda, and Abigail kept walking but at a slower pace as they passed the rest of the travelers. It didn't take Paul and Jack but a couple of minutes to catch up with the kids. "There's a slight change of plan. Believe it or not, the authorities are looking for twins. So, we are going to split up," Jack said. "Paul and Aaron are going straight to the boat."

Paul interrupted. "Abigail, I need you to do everything Jack tells you to do. I know how you feel, but this is of the utmost importance."

Abigail looked at Jack and then Miranda, and Miranda nodded.

"Abigail, if you cause a scene, all our lives will be in danger," Jack said.

"Two things, Abigail," Paul said. "You keep me magic wand, and you get both keys. You are to pretend to be Jacks prisoner."

Abigail had a pained and questioning look on her face. Jack handed her what looked like two skeleton keys. Abigail put one in her belt pouch and dropped the other down the side of her boot. Jack set down his bag, opened it, and pulled out a belt with a holster. He put it on. He also pulled out a gun and a set of handcuffs. He checked to make sure the gun was loaded. Then he put the gun in the holster. He handed the handcuffs to Miranda. Abigail pulled back and then slowly put her hands out in front of her. Miranda frowned but did as she was told, leaving them loose enough to slide out of.

Jack looked her in the eye and repeated. "I'm very sorry. You have both keys."

Paul spoke up. "And you have me magic wand. You already know how to use it. We are going to have to separate the twins, and there is no such thing as a free tree anymore. Miranda, put me harness and leash back on."

Jack directed, "Paul and Aaron are going to go straight to the houseboat. Abigail, Miranda, and I are going straight to the warehouse. We are going to put Miranda inside one of my barrels. I have a shipment of cider I am delivering to Queensland, so we will take her barrel with us." Jack turned and spoke to Paul and Aaron. "You will find the boat at the end of dock number seventy-three, just off Cherry Street on the southeast edge of Boston. I will be taking Abigail and

Miranda to a warehouse three blocks west. I will see everyone at the dock in an hour and a half. Don't waste any time. Don't stop moving."

"Give us ten minutes to get ahead of you. As soon as we are through the gates," Paul said, "then, Jack, you can follow."

Jack was right. The guards at the entrance to the city took some time asking Aaron questions. Paul and Aaron were allowed to enter. Within a few minutes, Paul addressed Aaron.

"I said to lie Aaron," Paul chastised. "Not to make up a stupid story involving me being some sort of racing goat. You are nuts, kid."

"Why? I liked it," Aaron replied with a grin.

"You could have gotten us busted!" Paul said. "Let us hang back to make sure the others get through. And take this stupid leash and harness off me!"

"That's not exactly what Jack said to do," Aaron said.

"Jack is working for me, not the other way around! I do not want to lose sight of your sister or Abigail," Paul stressed. The two walked slowly down the street, waiting to make sure Jack, Miranda, and Abigail made it through the gate. "Let us wait till they pass us and then follow them. Quick—in here."

Paul and Aaron slid through the front door of a little shop. Apparently, it was a pet store. It had that unique pet store smell. Aaron started to look around immediately. Paul was looking out the front window, waiting for Jack and the girls to pass by. As Aaron was distracted, he walked around the corner of the aisle. There were all sorts of treats and food. There was a large glass wall with hundreds of spiders about the size of soccer balls behind it. Apparently, they were babies, with a big old gray lumpy mama spider in the corner behind the glass. He turned and walked up to the counter, where a short bald man with a gray beard and glasses stood. The man wore a long orange and brown robe.

"What can I help you with?" the man asked.

By then, Paul had realized Aaron had wandered off and caught back up with him. "I'm just looking," Aaron said. Paul took a sharp look to the left and realized there was a fairy locked up in a cage over by the far wall.

The short bald man with the glasses came around the counter. "Would you like to see one of the spiders? They're on-sale. Spider pup for a silver star."

Aaron took two steps toward the spider enclosure. "We were just looking, and I'm just here with my goat. Besides, I don't have any money."

The man's demeanor changed like a candle being blown out. He squinted up at Aaron. "What? No money? No monies, no spiders! Out! Both of you!"

Paul rubbed the side of his head sideways across the counter, licking the counter. The man pushed Aaron toward the front door. Paul ran around the other aisle, past the fairy's cage. It looked as if Paul had spit on the fairy. Next, Paul slid past Aaron and out the front door.

Jack, Abigail, and Miranda had already passed; Paul could see the backs of the threesome in the crowd of pedestrians. Paul yelled back in Aaron's direction,

"Hurry up, and give us half a minute, some distance! Half a minute!"

The man had already pushed Aaron out onto the front stoop. He smacked his hands together as if he were dusting them off, shouting, "BE GONE! And don't waste my time again! No star, No spiders!" He walked back inside slamming the door as he went.

Aaron caught back up with Paul and asked, "What was that all about?"

"First off, do not leave me side again, and let us hurry, Aaron, because he is a wizard. Secondly, that was a fairy in a cage. I have never seen that before. That wizard is going to pay dearly now," Paul chuckled.

"But you spit on it."

"I did not spit on it. And it is a he, not an it. Do I look like I have hands? The fairy's magic wand was on the counter beside the wizard's hat. I licked it up and gave it back to the fairy."

There was the sound of an explosion along with a flash of light from half a block behind Aaron and Paul. Aaron realized it came from the pet store. Then a second explosion sounded. The front glass window shattered as a streak of light shot into the air.

"I wonder whether the old man ever saw it coming," Paul said with a pleased grin.

Paul also noticed Squeaks was flying in circles way up in the sky above the warehouses.

Aaron questioned, "Why doesn't she just fly down here?"

Paul watching her thought. *I bet Jack has double crossed us.* "I think we may be in for a surprise. HURRY, we can not loose sight of the girls," Paul responded.

Paul and Aaron were about a hundred feet behind Jack and the girls. Jack eventually made it to the warehouse not far from the docks. Paul and Aaron waited impatiently outside a couple doors down the street. Aaron was still watching Squeaks. After what seemed like forever, Jack and Abigail emerged. Abigail was carrying a large wooden barrel. They headed down the street toward the docks. Paul and Aaron followed. Ten minutes passed before Jack and Abigail walked out onto dock number seventy-three, where Jack kept his boat. Jack's houseboat was not small after all. It looked to be about forty-five to fifty feet long.

Jack and Abigail hurried up the ramp and onto the boat. Abigail set the large barrel down carefully. She fished in her pouch for the key and removed her shackles. Jack emerged again from below deck. Jack pointed to a dockworker who was moving more, large wooden barrels onto the dock. Jack and Abigail ran back down the ramp and worked together to load the drums onto the boat ahead of schedule. Jack didn't want to wait for more dockworkers to help load the cargo. Miranda climbed out of the barrel Abigail first brought onto the boat.

Paul yelled to Aaron, "We need to hurry up! Druid!"

Aaron looked around, and about fifty feet behind him was a Croatan druid. The druid looked to be closing in on them fast. Just as Aaron turned to run, he saw a rock headed straight for his head. He ducked just in time.

Sorry!

Paul and Aaron ran as Squeaks flew in the opposite direction, dropping rocks. It didn't stop the Croatoan druid, but it sure slowed him down. The Croatoan pulled out a large knife. Squeaks made sure to stay far enough away. She kept flying back to the shore, looking for anything she could find to throw at the Croatoan druid.

Aaron made it to the end of the walkway leading to the dock. Paul realized Aaron couldn't outrun the druid. He turned around, dropped his head into a full-tilt boogie, and ran back in the opposite direction, directly at the druid. The druid didn't have a plan for what was coming. Paul rammed him square in the chest. Paul bounced sideways; the Croatoan druid shot backward. He did not get up right away. Paul staggered around and headed for the boat.

Aaron made it to the ramp and was on the boat in no time. Paul made it up the ramp right behind Aaron and then collapsed on the deck. Paul's attack on the Croatoan druid had given Jack and Abigail time to load four more barrels onto the boat. Jack swore aloud and he and Abigail returned to the boat leaving a couple barrels behind.

The Croatoan druid got to his feet. He was staggering and looking around for his knife. He didn't find it. Shaking his head, he started down the dock. When he heard the engine, he pulled out a magic wand and started sending fireballs toward the boat.

Jack started the boat, backed the boat away while shooting his pistol blindly at the stranger. He was angry about leaving the barrels behind. Miranda and Abigail were prying at the knots in the ropes, trying to get them off the boat. The Croatoan realized what was happening and started to run, but it was too late. Abigail and Miranda were able to undo the ropes. Just as the boat backed away, turning toward the open waters of the bay, Aaron did an amazing but foolhardy thing. He found an orange box at the back of the boat marked, "Flare gun." He pointed it at the drums left on the dock and fired. The drums exploded, along with half the dock. The Croatoan druid found himself swimming for his life.

Jack didn't hold back. He headed for open water. They had made it. Squeaks landed on the deck. Everyone was hugging, patting each other on the back, while doing a victory dance.

Paul was slumped over beside the edge of the boat. Squeaks pointed to Paul. Apparently, the Croatoan had not missed after all. Paul had a deep laceration in the side of his belly, just behind his front leg.

Miranda ran up to Jack's bridge. She explained about Paul. He showed her how to steer the boat straight and then backed the throttle off a little, slowing the boat's speed. He told Miranda to keep it straight and went down to address Paul's situation.

Jack carried Paul inside and laid him down. Jack was able to clean and dress the wound at least enough to keep him from bleeding to death. He told Abigail to keep an eye on Paul and to keep him awake. He needed to get back to the bridge to relieve Miranda, so she didn't end up running aground where the sea ended and open river water began. He said he would be back once they got out into the main current.

The group had made their escape. Once they made it to open water, Jack went to check on Paul. He seemed to be doing a little better. Now that Jack had time to really check the wound, he saw that it was not as bad as he originally had thought. The cut was not quite as deep as he'd thought, nor was anything vital involved, but it was still a nasty wound and could easily get infected. "You're a brave man, Paul," Jack said.

Paul mumbled, "I mean to uphold me vow. I wonder how they knew we were there."

Squeaks spoke up. "The coach driver swung back around and let one of the officers at the wall know where you were headed."

"Good job, Squeaks," Jack said. "That dirty rotten Mayor Somerson. And why were you behind, Paul?" he asked.

Paul thought for a minute. "Just a precaution," he said. "I did not want to be stuck on the end of the dock with nowhere to go. When you first meet people, you do not put all your trust in them all at once. You give them a job and test that trust a few times. I have had many men serve under me command. You have done an amazing job today, Jack. Miranda said she trusted you. She was right. Now am I allowed to get some rest?"

"I think that will be fine," Jack said. "I'm going to put on some speed for a couple days, getting some distance from Boston's coastline. It's going to take us nineteen to twenty days to make it all the way around to Berlin. And I must also make a stop on the way. We all can get some rest for a little while."

CHAPTER 12

Paul and Jack's Understanding

FOR THE FIRST TIME SINCE PAUL HAD BEEN WOUNDED, he joined everybody at the table. Miranda had made a simple meal: peanut butter sandwiches with a side of chicken soup. Aaron kept following the stack of sandwiches. Squeaks flew in and sat down. She was ready to eat. Aaron eyeballed Squeaks.

Paul smiled. "Why so jumpy, Aaron?"

Aaron grinned. "You know," he mumbled.

Miranda interrupted. "I wouldn't do that intentionally to you! Although I'd probably let you do it to yourself again." She was pretending to be offended. Ever since the chunky cricket grilled cheese sandwiches, Aaron had taken to checking all his food. He had even accused the girls of trying to give him crickets a second time two nights ago, when they'd had grilled cheese sandwiches again.

Everyone burst into laughter. Still, Aaron picked up the corner of his bread to check it out. "One can never be too sure around this lot," he said.

Squeaks said, "One of these days, --*Squeak*-- I'll get me cheesy crunchies."

They all turned as they heard Jack coming down the steps from the bridge. "Turning out to be a pretty bright day. Still no sign of anyone other than a fishing and cargo vessel," Jack said. They hadn't seen many boats. "Paul, explain to me again why you have to stop off at the palace."

Paul quickly turned his head. "I thought I was being very clear, Jack. I must take the twins to the palace so I can be sure to bring good proof to the Senate, or we will have a heck of a time proving the kids' royal status."

"I know that's what you said," replied Jack. "I'm just worried about making my schedule. I've never been late before, and I really don't want to be. I could possibly have my permits pulled and checked for simply being late, and the boat might be inspected. And I certainly wouldn't want them to find any of my Appalachian apple cider."

Paul looked irritated. "We have had this argument before."

The kids were sitting there watching the exchange. It was like watching a tennis match.

Paul finally said, "I will give you more of me money."

Jack replied after taking a huge, deep breath, "Paul, although I like more money, it's a family problem, like I've said it before." He stood there looking at the cabin ceiling and paused. "Oh, very well, you might as well know. Money will not fix it. It's a supply-and-demand problem. Ollie's cousin Georgia needs the booze in Brisbane." Jack sat down and looked at his hands on the table. "She struggles because of oppressive taxes Queensland puts on the people of their cavern, especially on special sauces, like whiskey. She picks up her yearly supply in Melbourne—three or four barrels— and then returns with them to her tavern in Brisbane. Every year, we bring them two or three more barrels of cider from Appalachia. That pretty much gets her through the year despite the heavy taxes and the competition of her competitors. And I've picked up where Ollie left off, as he's getting older, and it is getting tougher for him to make the run. Because of our deliveries, she is able to survive and turn a decent profit."

Miranda finally spoke up. "We'll make it. It will be fine. We will stop at the palace quickly, and then we'll hurry on to the Queensland caverns. We'll be fine. We don't need to fight over stupid things."

After a few minutes, Jack said, "I know I'm just being worrisome. And it's not the first time I've had my boat searched. I've been doing this for Oliver for at least nine years, maybe ten. I'm pretty sure he was doing it for about a dozen years before that." Jack stood up and clapped his hands together. "Next stop the

Bay of Lights." He left the cabin and headed toward the bridge.

Aaron looked at Paul and spoke with a mouthful of sandwich. "Ho utt's a Cay of Ites?"

Abigail, who was sitting at the table across from him, looked at Aaron with her forehead all scrunched up. "How can you even talk? Gross! I can even see your sandwich." She shook her head.

After finally swallowing, Aaron repeated himself. "I said, so what is the Bay of Lights?" He shrugged. "I'm hungry. I'm always hungry."

Paul spoke up. "The Bay of Lights is a special place. It sits smack dab below Antarctica, which has no trees, so it never gets light. The fish down here, even dolphins and whales, have adapted. They have grown their own lights—bioluminescence. So, as we move across the water's surface, from time to time, you will see sparkly fish emerge from the depths of the water. Some have glowing streaks that run down their bodies, and some of them are neon green and hot pink, the glow-in-the-dark kind of colors. It is an amazing place. I have only ever seen it with me eyes one other time. The international community even limits the number of fishermen permitted to fish there. It takes a special license."

The kids hurried up eating. They decided to do the dishes together, so they all could get to the upper deck, and none of the group would be left out. Paul took the long way around and up the short steps at the back of the boat as the kids started the dishes. He was not able to use the ladder like everyone else.

When the kids were finally done with the chores and made it to the upper deck, Paul was relaxing on a lounge chair. Jack hollered, "Everyone hold on to something! It will get choppy when we leave the main current."

All the kids held on to the rail. Sure enough, the boat felt as if it were bouncing along the water sideways instead of smoothly sliding through it. It was like putting on the brakes. As the boat started to smooth out, Jack sped up again after he had entered into the open water of the bay.

As the houseboat got closer to the South Pole, Jack went up and turn on a special red light at the front of the boat. The cavern ceiling was getting dark. The roots of the cavern seemed to just come to an end. Within twenty minutes or so, everyone on the deck was standing in the black darkness. They could not see the waterway. It was like inky black soup. Off in the distance, the group could see lights sparkling on top of the water. They were all different colors. Squeaks took to the air. Paul yelled at her, "Do not go too far!"

"I won't," Squeaks replied.

Just then, a huge whale slid up out of the water, spraying the whole boat with its spout. It had thousands of little lights that glittered on its side.

Abigail, who seldom said anything, spoke. "This is amazing. That is the most magnificent creature I have ever seen. She is so beautiful." It was quite a sight.

It took them the better part of two days to leave the entrance and cross the bay, where they were approaching the docks. As they got closer to the Dundalk continental cavern shoreline, the group saw two lighthouses on opposite ends of the southern edge of the continental cavern. They headed toward the one to the right. The lighthouses seemed to drown out some of the lights of the fish. In the last two days, they had only passed three or four little fishing vessels. As they worked their way toward the shore, Jack pulled up and tied off to the dock.

Jack asked Paul, "How long do you think this will take? You know I'll be late."

"I know," said Paul. "And I am truly sorry. I think it will take us about two days if we make good time."

The group tied the boat off to the dock and then made it down to the shoreline. Jack wanted to join the group this time. He had never seen the inside of the palace. Jack also supplied everyone with an old-fashioned oil lantern. Everyone had plenty of light. Paul pointed out that as they approached the palace from the south, they would eventually see light again. They would be far enough away from the South Pole.

Most of the cities of this cavern lined the northern edge, except for one, Drogheda. The southern edge of the cavern was a barren place. It was a lot more like the tunnels the twins had encountered when they first left the world above. It was much rockier and dirtier, with no vegetation. But it wasn't cold. Aaron said, "Shouldn't it be cooler since we're underneath the South Pole?"

Jack replied, "No, caverns keep a constant temperature. The main river is four degrees cooler because of the airflow and the current of the water. All the other caverns stay the same: on average fourteen degrees Celsius, depending on the season."

The group quickly marched on. Jack seemed to be pushing them. It took them the better part of half a day. They realized they could see the palace off on the horizon, as well as the beginning of some daylight. They were coming upon a little bridge. Once they had crossed it, they came across a group of boys just on the other side of the bridge, to the side of the roadway.

Paul stopped for a minute by their fire. "And who do we have here?" he asked.

The boys did not seem to be taken aback by a talking goat. A tall boy spoke up. "My name is Curtis." He looked to be a couple of years older than the others. He had dusty-blond hair in a fishbowl haircut. He was wearing a long dark blue robe. The other three boys were also wearing blue robes, covered in patches.

Paul asked Curtis, "And how are your studies going, young man?"

"Good," Curtis replied, and he looked at the younger two kids. They just smiled.

"And where is your instructor?" Paul asked.

"He should be back in a day or so. Our professor took some potions with him he planned to trade with some gargoyles. There is a village not far from here. He needs more herbs from some of the northern caverns, and he figured the gargoyles may have some. Do you guys have anything you want to trade?"

The discussion of gargoyles and trading seemed to get Abigail's attention. "And where is this village?" she asked.

"There are two. One to the east and one to the west of this cavern. They both are in the dark lands, though," Curtis said. Talking to a tree didn't seem to bother Curtis. "There seems to be a lot more of you guys down here now as well."

One of the young boys spoke up. "The gargoyles have been keeping a lot more trees with them."

"Where is this village?" Paul asked. "Me young sapling here is looking for her parents."

"Me mum's name is Rachel Eberleaf, and me papa's name is Samuel Eberleaf. They have been taken, and I need to find them," Abigail said with concern.

The boy seemed more reserved now. "Well, you should probably ask our teacher, Professor VanDyne. He should be back in a day or so."

Paul said, "We are headed to the palace."

Jack, starting to seem impatient, asked the young man, "How far is the village from here?"

Curtis hesitated. "Just a couple hours to the east. Now I'm going to get back to my cooking. And we have lessons after lunch. Stop back tomorrow." Curtis went back toward the campfire and his cooking.

Jack, Paul, and the kids moved on toward the palace. The group moved up the road quickly. Jack was now pushing them again. In a couple of hours, they would be at the palace, but there was a problem again. The kids seemed to drop back during their forward march. They seemed to be quietly arguing among themselves.

Jack turned and looked back at the kids. "Why don't I see Abigail?"

Squeaks stopped short, pretending she didn't know. Her eyes got big.

Jack said, "Squeaks, go look," and she took off. She apparently wasn't going to stick around for this court-martial. Miranda and Aaron were left standing side by side, staring at their own toes.

Paul had backtracked, and he was now standing directly in front of the twins, staring up into their faces. "Where is Abigail?" he demanded, but neither of them answered. "Where is she? Where is Abigail? Do I have to take a head count every thirty minutes?"

Aaron spoke first. "I tried to talk her out of it."

Then Miranda said, "I told her she was being stupid and was going to get in trouble."

Jack said, "We're almost to the palace. Let's just pop in, test the twins, and catch her on the way back. We know she's headed toward the gargoyles' village."

Paul seemed about to flip into a rage. He pressed his lips together, speaking out of the side of his mouth while snorting hot air out his nose into Aaron's T-shirt. "We cannot do that, Jack."

"Why?" Jack asked.

Paul rolled his eyes. "Because Abigail has me magic wand. It would take the strength of thirty trained warriors to open the doors to the outer wall from the inside. Or a wizard with a magic wand, which I do not have at this moment."

Jack pressed his palms to his forehead. Paul walked around the twins, walking in a southward direction. Every so often, the group could hear Paul talking to himself, saying, "How could I be so stupid? I cannot believe I did not see that coming! I am such a fool. Omadhaun!"

Jack kept pushing the twins from behind, saying, "Keep up. Catch up to Paul. Move it."

After a while, Paul and Jack seemed to cool off some. Every so often, the twins could hear Paul say, "Gonna split me stitches. Gonna be the death of me. I simply have got to find her. I cannot lose her. She needs us. She is just a sapling. I refuse to let her down." Then he would push himself to go faster, which meant Jack would then push the twins to go faster.

The group made it back to the boys camping by the fire. The tall boy, Curtis, was not happy. He started yelling at Paul the second he saw him. "What in the earth is wrong with you people? That crazy stick of a girl just showed back up here an hour ago. She grabbed my magic wand, yanked it out of my hand, and threw it way over in the rocks. As I went to find it, she started tossing the young boys around. I gave up on looking for my wand. I tried to stop her."

Abigail had definitely gotten the best of Curtis. She had given him a bloody fat lip and a black eye that was already swollen shut. It had an ugly yellow and purplish black color to it.

Jack seemingly did not know what to say. Paul spoke up. "Curtis, I am truly sorry for me young lady friend. She is stressed beyond belief, to the breaking point. If I could do something to make this up to you, I would."

"Before she left us," Curtis said, "that bloody crazy twig took most of our food."

Jack quickly opened his pack and gave them all the food he had. The boys seemed to be content with the offer. One of the young boys spoke. "You should keep that one on a leash."

Paul said, "Which way did she go?" All the boys pointed. "Thank you very much."

The group headed over the bridge. Once they got to the other side, Jack stopped Paul. "Wait a minute. Squeaks, come down here for a minute."

It took a few minutes, but Squeaks returned. Squeaks had taken to flying circles about a quarter mile around the group, looking and listening. "I do not see her."

"That's okay," said Jack. "You're doing a good job. Let's split up. I'll take Miranda with me back to the boat. We will take the boat over to the docks near the second lighthouse. You can take Aaron and Squeaks. Check out this village, and then head to the other village. It makes more sense. That's where she's going to go. Splitting up will save you a trip back across the cavern when you find her. She is not a fool, and I'm also sure she's not going to find her parents at either of the villages."

Paul nodded. "I agree with you. I hate to split the twins up, though. I know Miranda will be safe with you. If Abigail's parents were taken from Appalachia, they certainly wouldn't be here; they would be in a work camp. It would be an unbelievable longshot. But I'm sure Abigail had to try." Paul didn't seem upset anymore. "I keep getting small, faint wisps of pine smell. She must be running pretty hard. She has got to be two, if not three, hours ahead of us by now. I just need to stay on her scent."

Jack handed his lantern off to Aaron, who now had two. "All I'm going to need is Miranda's. That will get us to the boat, and then you'll find our boat at the docks by the opposite lighthouse on the western coast of the bay."

"Sounds like a plan," said Paul. He then told Squeaks, "Keep doing your circle, and stay with us."

With a squeak, she was off again.

Miranda climbed up onto Jack's back piggy-back-style. She had one arm around his neck, and the other arm held the lantern off to the side. Jack started heading down the road at a brisk jog.

"Climb on, Aaron," said Paul, "but do not get used to it."

Aaron looked as if he were about to cry. "We can't lose her, Paul."

Paul responded, "We will not lose her. I promise you that. She is too much of a pain in me backside. We also know where she is going, Aaron."

Aaron seemed a little more relieved, and the two were off.

Within a couple of hours, Jack and Miranda were back at the dock. It did not take them long before they had the boat moving along the shoreline, heading straight across the Bay of Lights for the other lighthouse.

Meanwhile, Aaron and Paul came upon the north side of the gargoyles' village. They could see the glow of some torches. As Paul made it into the camp with Aaron on his back, they passed a few gargoyles, who seemed to be ignoring them. Aaron kept staring at them. He had never seen a gargoyle before. Some were tall and thin, and some were short and heavy. They were no different from regular people. Their dress was like that of American Indians. They wore short leather skirts kind of like kilts, as well as short-sleeved leather vests as shirts. They also wore leather sandals. Their feet were more like talons, bird feet. They had three large toes out in the front and one toe where their heel should be. Their hands were slightly different as well. They had three large fingers and one thumb. Their skin was dark gray like the color of a shark. They had horns like a goat's and long, thin tails. Despite all the differences, they still looked like people. They were not ugly. They had different-looking faces.

Paul stopped a couple of times to ask random gargoyles, "Have any of you seen a deciduous tree girl?" Most of the gargoyles did not speak English, but there were a few who could. They told Paul that a girl had run through and had talked to the other trees at the south side of the village.

Paul and Aaron found out that those trees were not from Abigail's clan. There were two families of trees on the outskirts of the village. They had large, round, mitten-shaped leaves. The vines on their heads were shorter. They were not like Abigail. The two men from the tree families spoke to Paul.

"We tried to convince her to stay with our families," said one tree.

The second tree then said, "It is not safe any-more. She'll probably get caught. It can even happen down here."

"We are living in fear," said the first tree.

"Why did she run off?" asked Aaron. "Why couldn't she just stay with us? We would help her."

"I know that is how you look at it," said Paul. "She has not quite figured that out yet. Even though she is with us, she still feels totally alone. We will catch her at the next village. Let us not waste any more time talking. I must catch back up to that smell of pine again."

Paul and Aaron continued straight west.

Late into the next night, Paul and Aaron made it halfway across the cavern and ran into a wall of stone, a pillar that supported the massive ceiling. Paul was still following the pine sent of Abigail. The twosome followed the wall in a southward direction toward the bay, and within an hour, they found a stone circle. It resembled one Aaron remembered from his history textbook, one called Stonehenge, a rock circle.

This circle had twelve large vertical rocks evenly placed. Six of which had odd looking markings in some

ancient language chiseled in the outer surfaces. The center of the circle of stone was empty. Paul walked around the circle. Once on the southern side the two could see a glow of a fire off in the distance.

Aaron said, "I hope that is the other village."

"I would put me monies on it," Paul replied. "Hop off of me back, it needs a break."

"She had better be there," Aaron said. "I need her to be there."

"Relax," said Paul.

Squeaks landed beside Paul and whispered in his ear.

"Very well. Thanks, Squeaks. Go let Jack know. Find the lighthouse. Jack will be at the docks closest to the lighthouse." Paul pointed out. "And, Aaron, do not start banging on in me ear. I have no desire to discuss your feelings." Paul smiled and headed toward the village.

It did not take long. Paul and Aaron made it into the village. The gargoyles there seemed just like the ones in the other village. They kept pointing toward a stone hut at the far end of the village. It was starting to sprinkle a little. There were two bushy-looking tree people leaning down, talking to Abigail. Paul and Aaron approached. Aaron kind of expected Paul to chew Abigail out, but he didn't.

"Augh, me young little sapling, been looking all over for me tree," Paul said.

Abigail was sitting there with her arms wrapped around her legs, crying with her face in her knees.

The young tree woman spoke. "We offered to keep her with us. It's not safe anymore."

Paul told the tree woman, "I know. But she is part of me clan now."

When Abigail heard Paul's voice, she looked up. Paul looked at her. "Apparently, this young prince has been looking all over the World Under for you. Now I think we have to catch a boat." Paul left Aaron standing there with Abigail as he started walking southwest toward the light of the lighthouse. It did not take long for the two kids to catch up.

"You know, Abigail, I think that caused a couple of me stitches to pop. I have me a scar because of you," Paul teased sternly.

Abigail just smiled. She had regained her usual composure.

It didn't take the threesome long to get down to the other dock. Squeaks were there. Miranda and Jack were waiting on the boat. Jack hollered, "Come on! I don't have all day. I've got somewhere I need to be. It will be the first time I've ever been late." He shook his head and went back to the bridge.

Within minutes, the kids had the boat free, and they headed south toward the bay entrance. Aaron could tell Miranda was irritated. She was ignoring her brother and hanging out with Jack by the bridge, and she seemed not to even want to talk or look at Abigail.

CHAPTER 13

The Reality about What Is Happening to the Trees

T HE NEXT FIVE DAYS PASSED QUICKLY. MIRANDA took a different approach: she acted as if everything were perfect. They had a lot of fun and played a lot of games. Everyone got along, and they all even took turns cooking. Paul had Squeaks fly reconnaissance missions, looking to see what close passing ships were transporting as well as listening to what the boats' crews had to say. None of it worked out; Squeaks came up short. There was no evidence or news of anyone looking for the twins. After a couple of days of missions, Squeaks seemed irritated when Paul called for her. She just wanted to hang out with the rest of her friends. Aaron developed a new game as a pastime: everyone would stand at the edge of the boat and take turns seeing who could get the flying disc the farthest out to sea. Then Squeaks would go retrieve it. Paul warned that the World Under had sharks and told Squeaks to be cautious: "Look before you leap, or you might be a cricket sandwich yourself." Squeaks said she could see a little bit below the water with her echolocation.

The closer they got to Queensland; the more paranoid Paul became. It was almost as if he were expecting something to happen. They were surprised when they got to the cove with smooth sailing. At that point, Jack cut back the engine power and yelled, "Hold on!" Everyone did as he advised. Squeaks took off. Everyone else had a seat or grabbed ahold of the railing.

Once they broke out of the river current, the water smoothed out. "This ceiling is really bright," Aaron said, looking up into the main root of the system. The twins were standing at the rail, staring into the massive city in front of them. Melbourne made Boston look tiny.

Jack laughed. "You could get lost in there, and it would take you forever to find your way out. Use the roots above to guide you in Melbourne. The streets run in circles like a spider web, not like other cities."

Melbourne seemed massive. In another couple of hours, the group would be beyond Melbourne, staring at another wall of rock that separated the sea from the land. The sea was amazingly bright; the roots that lined the ceiling were blinding. Aaron yelled, "Hey, look! Here come more fields!"

As the cavern passed by, all the kids, standing on deck, were amazed at the size of it. They couldn't see the far side of the sea, nor could they see the back side of Queensland. The grass died where the trees began and ran toward the horizon. Aaron and Miranda were poking each other and acting like typical siblings. Aaron was making faces. Squeaks was laughing and licking at her arms. Miranda kept sticking her tongue out at the two of them. Paul had found one of the large lounge chairs and was lying down, basking in the root light. Jack was up front, piloting the boat, which was a job Miranda now enjoyed. She had taken to volunteering to pilot the boat.

"Hey, Paul," Aaron said, "with there being millions of people down here, why wouldn't we know about it up there?"

"Most of the millions of people down here," Paul replied, "do not know that there is much up there, not to mention that there are very few tunnels to the surface. There is maybe a couple dozen at most, the majority are protected and guarded. Think about it: How long from the surface did we walk before we found light? Appalachia is one of the shortest trails."

"Two days," Aaron replied.

"Three and a half for our tunnel," Squeaks added.

"I guess that makes sense," Aaron said. Aaron always had questions.

The group could see the shore much more clearly. There were hundreds of coaches pulled by spiders moving back and forth up and down the coast. The group stood, leaning on the rails, taking in the scenery. "Soon we are going to see nothing but country. It will take a couple hours to get down to Brisbane," Jack said.

They all kept watching the scenery play out before their eyes. There were tons of farms. There were fields surrounded by rock walls, and goats and sheep were everywhere. The field grasses seemed much taller there than in Appalachia. The roots were much brighter. Aaron, always thinking, pointed out that they were much closer to the equator. "Never thought about that, Aaron," Paul said.

Suddenly, there was a second massive rock wall, and they couldn't see land anymore, just the cavern wall. "It will take about an hour before you'll be able to see the continental caverns land again," Jack said. The group went back to playing the flying disc game with Squeaks.

After an hour and a half, they were looking at more fields of grass. They started watching the scenery again, except this time, they were looking at rows and rows of crops: corn, beans, and strawberries. Occasionally, they saw a tall evergreen out there working, but no one gave it a second thought. Abigail seemed to pay close attention, though. They came upon an area of trees. It was a tree farm, an apple orchard. Abigail burst into tears and dropped to her knees.

Jack ran down the deck toward the group. Paul jumped to his feet and was in a full-tilt boogie toward Abigail simultaneously. Jack yelled out something about getting her wand before she did something stupid. Paul stripped her of the magic wand with his mouth before she could even think. She lay there shaking and pointing. Jack told Squeaks, "Take over on the bridge! Keep the boat parallel to the shoreline." Squeaks took off.

Aaron stood in horror, and Miranda dropped to her knees beside Abigail. Miranda was comforting Abigail, and Aaron was staring wide eyed at the shoreline. The group had been watching the workings of a slave camp. The trees were being forced to pick the apples. There were men on spiders everywhere. It was a solemn scene. The guards walked up and down among the trees, constantly keeping an eye out, making sure the trees were working hard like they were supposed to be. Aaron turned and looked at Miranda; his eyes were full of silent tears. Aaron looked at his sister and kicked the makeshift flying disk off the edge of the boat.

Paul took control. He spit his magic wand down onto the boat deck. "Everybody downstairs," he commanded. "Everybody below deck quickly. Aaron, pickup me wand." Paul commanded.

The entire group moved below deck. Miranda helped Abigail navigate the steps of the ladder. Instead of Paul taking the usual long way around to use the short steps, Jack picked him up and carried him. Paul grumbled to himself as he got down below. Jack decided to give the group some privacy and headed back to his bridge. "I'm going to relieve Squeaks," he said.

It wasn't long before Squeaks returned to the group. Abigail and Miranda were sitting on a small, cushioned sofa. Aaron was sitting by himself at the table with the magic wand in one hand. His other hand was clenched into a fist. The tip of the wand was glowing red.

Paul addressed Aaron. "Put me magic wand down before you blow up the ship and do something stupid that you did not intend to do!"

Abigail's face was drenched in tears. She had her arms wrapped around her shins, and her forehead resting on her knees. She was still shaking. "I am never going to find them! I am never going to find me parents!"

No one knew what to say. Miranda kept stroking her viny hair. Squeaks snuggled up against the other side of Abigail and folded a wing around both girls. Paul lay down, putting his chin on Abigail's boot and stared up at the threesome.

Wham. Aaron banged a fist on the table. "If we live through this and I ever become king, I will see every last tree free and make those who caused this evil pay dearly!" He continued to stare out the port window.

CHAPTER 14

A Quick Switch

PAUL AND JACK HAD A MEETING. THE KIDS WEREN'T included. That type of adult exclusion always irritated Miranda. Squeaks was included in the meeting this time. When Squeaks was called to join the meeting, she winked at Miranda. Aaron said, "Let me guess. Reconnaissance?"

"Yup," Miranda replied.

Jack took the boat around in large circles out in the middle of the sea. Squeaks came back. The dockworkers had been talking about a nosy wizard, most likely a Croatoan druid. They were also looking for a bootlegger in the company of a goat. There was no mention of the kids.

Jack now had the boat on autopilot. Squeaks was off again.

"Now where is she going?" Aaron asked Miranda.

In a couple of hours, Squeaks returned. She went straight to Jack, talked to him, and then joined the group below deck. Paul kept looking at Squeaks. Finally, Paul, irritated, stamped his foot, got up, and left the room. "Go ahead and tell them! You are going to anyhow!" he said. The kids could hear Paul as he headed down the hall. "Blasted downright nosy some would say. Simply rude."

As Paul went off into the distance, Squeaks finally spoke up. "I don't think he cares that we know; he's just a grumpy old goat."

"Tell us," Aaron said. "Are we docking?"

"Kinda," Squeaks replied. "We are not going to the docks. They are looking for us."

Abigail looked at the twins and gave them a small smile. She was clearly still struggling with what she had just seen.

"I talked to Georgia, Jack's future cousin-in-law. She and another fellow are going to join us out here in the sea. We're going to use the second boat as a decoy. I think we are staying on this one. Jack's boat, I found out, it is much faster, not to mention that Georgia needs her fishing vessels. The year has been a tough year for her," Squeaks said.

After Squeaks had filled them in on the plan, the group went up on deck. Paul was lying on his usual lounge chair, basking in the glow of the root. Paul looked at Squeaks. "I want you to fly out to greet them and then come back. Make sure they do not have any guests we do not want to see. In fact, do not land; just do a flyby."

Squeaks did as Paul asked. She was back in ten minutes. "All safe."

It took another half hour for the boats to arrive. They loaded the barrels of whiskey into a rowboat that was tethered to the back of one of the fishing vessels. That boat headed off toward the pixie cliffs on the opposite side of the sea. There was a large wall where most of the pixies lived. They had tiny caves the whole way up and down the coastline, on the opposite side of Queensland Bay. Pixies and fairies were not like people; they were creatures unique to themselves. They claimed no loyalty to any underground group. In years past, witches and wizards had tried to deal with them much like the evergreens and gargoyles, but enslaving pixies and fairies was not an easy thing to do. They had magical abilities. Pixies carried bags filled with magic powder. Fairies had their own magic wands. They could use their magic wands and magic dust to cause people to fall asleep. If someone got too close, it was lights-out. Years ago, some fishermen had tried to catch them. Falling asleep in the water did not work out well for the fishermen.

Georgia was having the fishing boat leave all the Appalachian cider in the rowboat, tied to a rocky ledge beneath the caves. She would come back for it in a couple of days.

"Do the fishermen have to worry about the pixies?" Aaron asked.

Paul chuckled. "No, as long as they are not stupid enough to try to catch them. A tied-up rowboat is not a bad idea either. Most fishermen avoid the pixies' coastline."

Just then, Georgia's boat pulled up beside the houseboat, and they tied off.

Georgia was a tall woman with deep red hair. She was clearly older than Jack. She had lots of little wrinkles around the corners of her eyes. Jack boarded the fishing vessel to give Georgia a big hug and kissed both of her cheeks.

Georgia spoke with an Italian accent. "I miss you so much! It's a shame I only get two hugs a year, and that's if I'm lucky!" Before she departed, she came aboard the houseboat with Jack to meet the twins. She gave them a small curtsy. "You both look very much like your parents. Of course, I've only seen them in pictures."

Miranda and Aaron looked at each other. Aaron shook his head. "I just can't get my mind around that."

"What?" asked Jack.

"The whole stupid notion of people bowing. It seems silly. We're just kids!"

Jack replied, "Yes, but you are going to be the hope for many—and a curse for some."

Paul lazily waddled up. "And a pain in me big, fat buttocks until that happens. And you know what falls out of there!"

His comment was enough to break the tension and even got a half smile from Abigail. Squeaks was rolling on the floor. *Giggle, Squeak, Giggle, Giggle.*

Jack shook his head. "We need to go. I'm actually going to pour some fuel into the engine this time around. They know where we are. They will be waiting for Georgia's fishing boats to return. They may even have a Queensland naval vessel looking for us at the entrance to the Great International River. Georgia is going to take a little extra time and do some fishing. That might give us a couple extra hours' head start. I was going to try backtracking out of the entry port, but now I think I'm going to hit the exit running. If there is anyone there, they are going to have to catch us. We're headed straight for Berlin—no stops and no slowing down. I'm going to keep the engine humming the entire way, even with the river currents. You guys have a date with the tribes. Since I have gotten to know you a bit, I don't think the tribes will be disappointed." Jack walked up toward the bridge. "And, Squeaks, no flying. You won't be able to keep up."

Within a few minutes, the boat was gliding right along, as if it were flying. Miranda looked at Aaron. His eyes were as big as baseballs. Squeaks had taken to holding on to whatever was in reach. "I don't like boats anymore," she complained. She was as excited as the twins, just not in a positive light. Abigail pointed at Squeaks, who was now closing her eyes in fear. The wind from their speed kept grabbing at her wings, trying to pull her off the deck as if she was wearing a parachute. The boat was not just moving along; it was skipping along the water. Apparently, Jack had put in a speedboat engine a couple of years back when he started delivering packages to his future cousin. It proved to be a good thing, because as they got close to the exit onto the Great International River, they spotted a couple of Queensland navy boats. They were not close to the exit yet. The navy blew their horns, but the group on Jack's boat didn't hesitate. They popped through the exit into international waters. The boat felt as if it would tip onto its side between leaving the smooth sea entrance and hitting the never-ending current of the oceanic river. In a few seconds, the boat smoothed itself out.

Jack did not stop the engines. He kept the boat moving. He hollered for Miranda to come to the bridge, and she did. "You can help with my steering, but I'm not going to let you have a go at it by yourself just yet. I want you to get the feel of controlling the boat at this speed with me by your side. You never know what surprises could happen when piloting."

Miranda was in heaven.

"After a while, we will slow down a little, but we will manage a decent clip until we get to Berlin. I do not understand how they keep getting ahead of us. It doesn't make sense," he told Miranda. "We are going to drive day and night, taking turns. I think we can be there in four and a half to five days. It would normally take six to seven days to make the trip."

Jack sent Miranda to bring Aaron to the bridge. He had both of them steer the boat together, and he slowed to three-quarters power. "Even if the Queensland navy is after us, this is the pace they would run, which means we will stay ahead of them."

The twins looked at each other and burst into laughter. Jack stayed with them for another hour or two and then went over to the side of the bridge, lay down on a little cot, and slept for five hours.

When Jack got up, he sent everyone to bed. "What a day," he said as Aaron was leaving the bridge behind Miranda. "Tell Abigail I'm truly, very sorry."

Aaron stopped at the cabin door, nodded in agreement, and then went on through.

CHAPTER 15

Lily's Asylum

THE GROUP ARRIVED AT THE SEA OF NESSIE. IT WAS A unique sea, as it shared shorelines with five separate countries: London, Berlin, Italy, Black Forest, England, and the Scottish/Irish Wizard Caverns were accessible through tunnels to the north. It was about midnight. There was a bit of glow to the root above, which meant the world above was experiencing a quarterly moon. They could just barely see. Paul said, "This works out well for me. As a goat, I can see fairly well in the dark."

Aaron chimed in through a big yawn. "Those weird-shaped eyes of yours give me the heebie-jeebies."

Squeak, Giggle, Giggle, "Of course, Heebie-Jeebies" said Squeaks, giggling.

Normally, Abigail stayed fairly quiet, but she slipped up for a change. She had just taken a large gulp of milk. Between her snickering and swallowing, milk came out her nose.

"Gross," Miranda said, brushing the milk off her right leg. Squeaks went nuts at this.

Jack powered the boat down to an idle. "We're out far enough. Nobody can hear us where we are. Squeaks, I want you to fly to the coastline. Then come back and let us know if anyone is there. Could you do that, please?"

"It will take about an hour." Squeaks popped up onto her two legs and gave a salute of some sort. "Aye, aye, Captain."

Aaron lost it again. Paul stamped his foot.

The group were lounging around in Jacks living room, relaxing. Paul spoke up again. "This is serious, and I need your attention. We will send Squeaks to check and see if we have any unwanted company on the coastline. This is what I am proposing. The witches are not necessarily going to be welcoming to the twins. They do not believe in World Under politics the normal way. They have their own political structure among the tribes. In other words, they do not agree with or conform to the World Under Government. The government tolerates them because they simply do not want to war against them. I believe the government would start a war if they thought for sure it would be a success, but it would be very costly for the government, and possibly, they could lose. I believe any skilled witch could take out a couple hundred men in an all-out battle, if not more. Would you be willing to attack with those odds? So, the government leaves the witch tribes and the witch lands alone. The witches will not bow down to the Senate or, worse yet in their viewpoint, another monarchy. That means you."

"Then why are we here?" Miranda asked.

"Me," said Paul. "I have business here. I took you to me cottage in the hope it would be a safe place. After running into Abigail and hearing what was going on with the tree clans, I feared much worse. That was when I knew there would not be a safe place for you anywhere out of the public's view. Me hope was that the two of you would be able to quietly enjoy some privacy in your lives, at least until you became adults. You could then deal with all of this as adults."

For once, Aaron wasn't screwing around. He was paying attention.

"Make me a promise Jack," Paul said. "If I do not return in three days, take the twins back to the gargoyle village."

"I promise," Jack said.

"The witches, for the most part, want nothing to do with the two of you. I married Lily and took her from the tribes. They excommunicated Lily. For the most part, she has been shunned. I am hoping that any family and her tribe will take her back. I am a wizard, so me loyalty is to the wizard guilds. The guilds will support me. The witch tribes are angry with me because I left with Lily and took employment with the previous king and queen. We have to be very careful, or we will lose the witches. This is really about our safest place. I will go talk to them meself."

The kids broke into arguing, pointing, and squawking.

"If you're going, we're all going. We are not staying here by ourselves!" Miranda shouted.

"Yes, you are," Paul said.

Miranda crossed her arms and stomped her foot. Aaron had an angry look on his face and gave a look of defiance in Paul's direction. "Just so you know," Aaron said mildly, "we swim quite well."

"Like fish," Miranda said with a smirk.

"Oh no you will not," Paul replied.

"Remember, you're a goat," Miranda said. "Do you really think you are going to out swim us?"

Paul snorted. "Yeah, I am still your boss. Me orders are final! Both your heads may be swelling at the idea of who you are. But I am about to pop them. I do not care what your title is; until you are of legal age, it does not matter. At that point, you can hang me from the gallows, but until then, I am going to be a royal pain in your—"

Jack jumped in. "I have a question. I stand before a talking goat. What makes you think the witches are just going to take your word for it?"

"Good point," Miranda and Aaron said simultaneously.

The group were quiet for a minute. *Tap. Tap. Tap. Tap. Tap.* Abigail had dropped into the recliner at the end of the coffee table. She kicked her feet onto the table while tapping Paul's magic wand against it.

"Brilliant!" Paul said. Apparently, at the cottage, Lily had told Abigail that Paul's wand had been a wedding gift from herself and one of her aunts. It had been grown there, deep within the tribal territory near her hometown. "That wand is the key, lassie. I just do not want anybody to sneak off." He eyeballed the twins. "So, if you would kindly pass that down here, I can get ready to go address the witches."

"Nope."

Everyone turned and looked at Abigail, who had been sitting there in silence.

"I have a question," Abigail said. "Do the tribes have anything to do with what is happening to me tree clans? If not, then it is the safest place for me as well."

"We know how well you can use your magic wand without one of us," said Miranda. "Looks like the big, dumb goat is going to have to give in."

Paul looked at Miranda and snorted. "You No!" He then looked at Abigail, who was smiling from ear to ear. "Very well, young lassie. You have a date. Jack can take us to the end of the dock, where Abigail and I will get off."

"It's going to take a couple hours to get there slowly and quiet," Jack said.

"We will head into the tree line, and you can follow me to the dancing fields," Paul said.

After the last couple of weeks of practice, Abigail was getting good at picking up small objects using the magic wand.

Aaron spoke up. "I'm going too."

Miranda stomped her foot.

Abigail smiled and said, "Nope, just me and the stinky one." She headed out of the room as she pointed at Paul.

"Me? Stink? You smell like pine!" Paul followed her out, saying the discussion was over.

Squeaks made it back within an hour. Jack filled Squeaks in on what was going on.

"Nothing to be seen on the shoreline," Squeaks said.

Jack had also ordered Squeaks to snitch if the twins tried to leave the boat.

CHAPTER 16
The Growing Fields

THE HOUSEBOAT CREPT UP TO THE END OF THE DOCK. Two figures hopped off the boat silently as it slowly slid by. Under the glow of the root, they headed toward the tree line. Abigail's beautiful greenish skin would blend into the forest quite well.

"Let us hurry," said Paul.

He and Abigail moved quickly down the dock and across the rocky shore. It took them at least ten minutes to reach the tree line. They disappeared into the darkness of the trees.

"I guess I am up for a workout," stated Paul, and Abigail hopped up onto his back.

The two figures moved quickly through the trees. Abigail could hardly see anything. Apparently, Paul could see fairly well with his oddly shaped goat eyes. They moved at a decent pace.

"I remember when I was a young wizard sneaking through here time and time again," Paul chuckled.

"You? Young? Oh yeah, I forgot," Abigail said. "That picture of you and Lily on the wall of the living room. You could not have been much older than we are."

Paul said, "I think I was about seventeen." He got quiet. "Shhh," he said, and he picked up the pace.

After a few minutes, Abigail asked, "What are you worried about?"

"Good question, Abigail," Paul replied. "It is one you need not worry about. Come to think of it, I do not remember spiders ever bothering a tree, but I have been wrong before. As for me, I have an ample amount of goat flesh for them, and me wand's ability has diminished some. So far, our eight-legged friends are far enough away that we are safe. We are going to keep moving and hope for the best."

Within an hour, the two emerged into a clearing. As they started across, they noticed there were a dozen crawling figures not far behind them. Paul kept moving forward between a fast trot and a slow run. "They are going to catch us. The question is, can we get to the witches before that happens?" Paul said.

"Look," Abigail said. They could see rows of grapevines up ahead.

"Wine is one of the largest and best products the tribes make. They like their wines," Paul said. "They are very much a capitalist group."

The spiders had closed about half the distance now. Paul headed down one of the rows in the vineyard.

They could hear women singing and see the glow of a fire off in the distance. The spiders had closed the distance to about fifty yards.

"Hold on to me horns, Abigail. This is it. Let us see who is faster." Paul leaned forward and pushed off into one of his full-tilt boogies.

The spiders shot forward, following his aggressive move. Paul bolted in an all-out sprint for the bushes and the fire that lay beyond. Abigail released one hand. She pulled the wand from her belt. It was hard to see, but she kept picking up clumps of dirt and flinging them backward toward the spiders the way a bride flung their bouquet: not necessarily aiming but hoping for the best. They rammed their way through the bushes. They made it. They crested the line where light met darkness in the witches' bonfire.

The witches turned to look at the absurd tree bouncing up and down on the back of a goat, heading straight for the chief witch. Instantly, they found themselves frozen in place. Apparently, the spiders had been around long enough to know where to stop. The spiders stood at the edge of the firelight, where it met the field's darkness. They turned and slowly melted away into the darkness.

"What might we have here, girls? This is shaping up to become quite an interesting evening or at least entertaining. It's not like this happens every day." The field filled with a lot of cackling and laughter. "There aren't many people either smart enough or stupid enough to jump out of the frying pan into the fire. You two had better make this good, or you will wish those spiders had caught you!" the chief witch said with a witchy, giggly cackle.

As quickly as the air had constricted around them, suddenly, the pressure released. Paul flopped down. Abigail slid off to the side and found herself lying in the grass. She still couldn't see well. She was now blinded by the fire's bright light. They were still a little way away from the fire.

Paul spoke. "It is I, Sir Paul Andrew Scott McTrustry, Lily's husband."

Everyone was quiet. The witches had formed a circle around the new arrivals.

The chief witch spoke. "What in the earth, after all these years, would cause you to consider showing your face here again after what you have done?"

Abigail shot Paul a sideways look. This could not be good. The witches went from simple entertainment and intrigue to all-out anger at the sight of Paul.

"And you are a furry little goat!" the chief witch said.

"Yes, Your Highness Chief Moon Bird," Paul replied. "I request your audience in a matter of great urgency concerning Lily and Emma." He kept his head bowed.

The chief witch spoke again. "Enlighten me, GOAT, before I feed you to the spiders."

"Your good friend Emma is with her husband, Edward, on the surface. They have been attacked. I quickly went to Lily's side to request her help for Emma. Emma was severely injured in an automobile accident caused by a druid attacker."

"You went to Lily's side? Explain," the chief witch said.

"I have not been with Lily for the past ten years," Paul said.

The statement seemed to invite everyone's interest. "That makes sense. She came to her senses," someone in the crowd said.

Paul continued. "She took me story for a lie. She attacked me and turned me into a goat."

"And yet you say you have seen her? Even though she turned you into a goat?" the chief witch said.

"Yes, she stayed at our home. I found her where I left her."

The statement seemed to irritate the chief, as Lily had not returned. "What proof do you have?" she demanded.

"I am standing before you a humble goat with a tree at me side knowing I am at your mercy. I came to you asking for help," Paul pointed out.

"You came running in and interrupted one of our private gatherings," the chief witch said. "The witches take their privacy and secrecy very, very seriously."

Abigail started feeling around her waist and looking around. One of the younger witches quickly walked up beside her and asked, "What are you looking for? Are you looking for this?" The witch displayed Paul's wand.

"Yes, I dropped it when I fell over onto me side."

One of the witches to the right of the chief looked over and said, "Let me see that!"

The young witch took it to her and presented the magic wand.

"My goodness, this wand was grown right here in this very field. It was sung from this very soil. It looks very much like Lily's work."

"Lily and a couple of her friends sang that magic wand as a wedding gift for me," Paul said.

"Enough of this," Shouted Chief Moon Bird. "State your purpose."

"Lily requests safe haven among the witches again. For herself and her aunt and uncle as well as their stepchildren. I also request safe passage and business dealings with the tribes again as Lily's estranged husband, along with any companions I accompany."

The chief stared at Paul. "Why should we grant such a request?"

A middle-aged witch strolled up toward the chief and bowed slightly. "I, Scarlett, speak for my sister, confused as she was. I request asylum for Lily and her family, by a motion of sanctuary."

The chief looked at her. "I knew you would, Scarlett. You have a kind heart—too kind possibly."

Another young witch stepped forward. "I, Jillian, second that motion. I wasn't much more than a child, but I do remember Lily. She was always so kind to me. Because Lily has a big heart and Scarlett believes in her so, I support Scarlett in this motion of sanctuary."

A third witch walked up. She was older and had a kind face but a stern look. "I, Ms. Blue, forward that motion of sanctuary. And offer it with what little properties I can spare. That will at least keep our visitors far enough away from our normal activities."

The chief looked up at the root as if she were seeing the moon itself. "I will grant such request." She raised her wand and pointed it toward the root. "So, what does my little spy have to offer?" The chief pulled the little bat slowly out of the air and set Squeaks down directly beside Paul.

Paul looked at Squeaks. Squeaks didn't say a word.

The chief addressed the group. "I suggest you three move quickly." She looked at Ms. Blue. "Take your apprentice and our so-called guests, Ms. Blue, and escort them back through the woods, where you can make them welcome on your lands." Chief Moon Bird looked at Paul, Abigail, and Squeaks. "I suggest you never, ever interrupt any of our private gatherings again, because your lives could depend on it."

Ms. Blue headed south. Paul muttered under his breath, "We need to quickly catch up with her and grab me magic wand."

Abigail retrieved it from the witch who had inspected it. Ms. Blue walked quickly beside her apprentice in a straight southward direction. No one spoke. The two witches made it through the woods and straight through another tree line, which put the two in a new grassy field. They were standing beside a large brick house, the home of Ms. Blue. Paul nodded, motioning for Ms. Blue. The two walked off to talk among themselves for some time. As Paul spoke, Ms. Blue's attention grew more intense, and her eyes got bigger and bigger.

"Royal twins. You tricked the tribe of witches into accepting the royal twins. Safe sanctuary for the royal family. I don't know whether you will go down in history or whether you will die a painful death as a dumb goat. This is going to start the tribes' fighting all over again. That hasn't happened for a couple hundred years!"

"I know," Paul said. "It was the only thing I could do. The whole Senate—the whole World Under—is looking to capture the twins and possibly execute them for being who they are."

Ms. Blue retorted, "Maybe that would have been best for the witches."

Ms. Blue raised her eyebrows. "I don't think I'm going to rush right back to offer up this additional information to the elders at this point. I think it would be best if no one said a word about who they really are. I will talk to the chief privately tomorrow night. And you say this one has some magical ability?" she said, pointing at Abigail.

"Oh yeah, a tree with magical ability. That is the reason she is holding me wand. I cannot use it very well. She seems to be quite gifted," Paul said.

"Miss Alissa, take our guests to the coastline, where they can gather their companions. Take seven other apprentices to give our guests an armed escort, but do not tell the girls why or who our guest are."

"Yes, ma'am." Alissa ran off.

Ms. Blue motioned for Paul and Abigail to have a seat on her porch. She then pointed to Squeaks. "You may go inform your friends to meet the girls at the dock and they are not to share who they are with the girls."

Squeaks took to the air.

CHAPTER 17

Results of Ms. Blue's forwarding motion

IT WASN'T LONG BEFORE A SMALL GROUP OF GIRLS RANGing in age from seven to fifteen gathered. Alissa addressed Paul and Abigail. "We're all here, so let's get moving." Some of the girls yawned.

Abigail spoke quietly to Paul, barely whispering in his ear.

Paul replied quietly, "No, you do not have to worry about the fact that they are just kids."

A couple of the younger ones turned and looked at them but didn't say anything. Paul chuckled and joked, "You know, young ladies, running into you in a dark alley with me pockets full of sweets would probably be bad for me." A couple of the girls giggled. "Nor, would it be wise for Miss Abigail to take an apple from any of these girls." The girls giggled again.

One of them offered Paul an apple, and he graciously took a bite. "Oh, I feel so woozy," he said, pretending to stagger around a bit as they walked. The girls giggled some more. Abigail laughed as well.

"Abigail, I think you hurt me spine running from those spiders. These old bones just are not what they used to be. Come to think of it, most goats only live about twelve years. I am almost there. I wonder how long this stupid curse will last. Could you imagine sixty years of arthritis?" Paul shook his head, and the girls giggled again.

During their march to the shore, Abigail swore she could hear spiders in the distance. She would see glimpses of a hairy leg or a set of eyes blink, but nothing approached. "Nervous, kid?" Paul asked.

Abigail looked at Paul, and Paul looked at Abigail. "I hope we never have problems with them again," she said.

"I do not think we will," Paul replied, "but they will not forget your throwing dirt into their eyes. You definitely know how to make friends. First you attack Jack, then Curtis, now our eight-legged friends."

The group crested the tree line. "Sure enough, it looks like we have guests," Paul said. Paul, Abigail, and the eight young ladies walked right past two strangers. "Hello, gentlemen." Paul nodded at the two large, ugly men. The two strangers skulked off into the distance toward one of the far docks.

The group could hear the motor of the houseboat humming as it headed toward the dock. It took about five minutes for the houseboat to show up and another ten minutes until they were properly docked. The two strangers never approached again, but they were avidly watching.

Jack reminded Paul that his job had come to an end. He agreed to wait for two more days out in the center of the bay. Jack also had a short conversation with Abigail in private. She refused to share any of the information from the conversation with the others, but she did show the twins a neat little multicolored wooden box Jack had given her. It had something jingling inside it. It was no larger than Aaron's palm. Aaron couldn't figure out how to open it, which made Abigail feel happy.

It took about half an hour for the group to gather their packs. They were ready to head toward Ms. Blue's. Miranda and Aaron kept asking the young witches questions, which they answered most of the time. Abigail was now quiet. She kept watching Aaron interact with the witches.

It wasn't long before the group were back at Ms. Blue's house. Ms. Blue dismissed the girls and thanked them for their time. She told them they only needed to show up for the second half of their lessons tomorrow and reminded them that there was still going to be a test on Friday. They went in different directions, leaving Ms. Blue's courtyard.

Ms. Blues home was a large brick house that had been painted purple. Inside it looked more like an old 1800's one room schoolhouse. The group found themselves standing in a large living room. There was an odd pungent fruity smell. The main room had been filled with desks and tables. The desks were arranged in three rows of five and the three tables were spaced down one side. On the tables were rows of beakers, test tubes and all sorts of shinny neat tools and stirs. On the opposite side of the room, built into the brick wall, were three fireplaces with burning fires. The smell was coming from the cauldrons that hung in them. In the rear of this amazing room sat a sofa and a staircase beside a door. The stairs went to a balcony with doors leading off. The door beside the stairs went to the kitchen.

Ms. Blue addressed the group. "While in my house, you must observe my rules."

The twins remembered their stern, strict reading instructor from school, Mrs. Gillian. No one ever crossed Mrs. Gillian.

Ms. Blue continued. "Squeaks, please stay for a moment. I want you to hear all the rules."

An old bat fluttered down and stood beside Squeaks. The whole group looked straight up. There was a large cupola in the center of the roof.

"I have a bat keep up there. There is room enough for three bats. You will have plenty of room, Squeaks. This is Mr. Toad."

Croak. The old bat with gray fur nodded. He wasn't young, smooth, or good-looking like Squeaks. He had a smooshed face with a lot of wrinkles. His eyes were milky white and possibly didn't even work. He was missing a large chunk of his left ear and two fingers on his right hand.

"Now, group, pay close attention. While you are staying at my house, you must follow my rules. You can be guests here if you follow them. The first rule, the biggest rule: young misters are not welcome in any of the other bedrooms. You're only welcome in the living room, the dining room, kitchen, and the courtyard. You are only allowed to use the facilities after you first knock and then count to four out loud!"

Aaron looked sideways at Alissa.

"Young boys and girls do not share private spaces under my roof for any reason. Paul, you may have the run of my property. Please keep this young mister in line."

Paul said, "Witches do not believe men to be very trustworthy."

Ms. Blue waited for a few seconds, cleared her throat, and then continued, "The second rule is my touching rule. As you can see, I am always working on potions and salves, some take as long as five moons to mature, none of which any of you will touch. I do not need my house to smell bad."

The twins looked at each other.

Ms. Blue cleared her throat again. "Nor do I need a gaping hole blown through the side of it. That would upset me. I don't think you want to upset me."

Alissa let out a little giggle.

Ms. Blue pointed her magic wand at the center fireplace, *fa's,* and flames grew and shot up around the cauldron hanging in the burning fire. Ms. Blue then gave Alissa a sharp look. Alissa stopped smiling and looked down. "The third rule: when I am not here, Miss Alissa and Mr. McTrustry are in charge." Miss Alissa was a girl that looked like she was about fifteen. "Our guests are not permitted to wander throughout the witches' territories. You are to stay here in the courtyard—nowhere else. That is important. While you are here, you are in a safe space, my space. Anywhere else, you could possibly find yourself in some rogue witch's stew."

Aaron and Miranda looked at each other with wide eyes. "You mean a witch would eat us?" Miranda asked.

Paul chuckled. "Possibly," he said.

"Toad, if you would, show Squeaks the perch," Ms. Blue directed.

Toad flew up to the perch in the cupola, and so did Squeaks. They were both asleep in minutes.

Ms. Blue said, "Toad sleeps so much that another bat around should be good for him. Miss Alissa will show Miss Abigail and Miss Miranda to your bedroom. Master Aaron, you are welcome to the sofa."

"I see a spot over by the fireplace where I can see the front door and the stairs to the girls' quarters on the second level," Paul said. "Come on, young man. Ms. Blue is not one for having her rules broken. I think she will permit you to use the end table beside the sofa to store your personal items."

Ms. Blue gave a nod and a small smile of approval. "I shall return to the kitchen to make chicken and dumplings for everyone," she said.

The group enjoyed a simple but filling dinner that night. Aaron found out talking to Ms. Blue that there were many different ways to cook mushrooms. He asked Ms. Blue a lot of questions. She seemed happy to answer him. Ms. Blue was fairly quiet but seemed to enjoy the large group of guests she had acquired.

After dinner, Miranda and Aaron explained to Ms. Blue what life on a farm was like. Alissa seemed interested in the information about the over world as well. They told Ms. Blue all about Grandma Emma and Grandpa Eddie. After the kids had made fools of themselves with a short game. Ms. Blue had them all turn in for the night. Tomorrow would be a new and exciting day.

CHAPTER 18

The Witches' Direction

T HE KIDS WERE ALLOWED TO SLEEP LATE THE NEXT morning. Aaron realized it was going to be just like the farm, maybe worse. He had to share a bathroom not only with his sister but also with two other young girls. After waiting for two hours, he had to pee and wasn't able to hold it any longer. Paul pointed his nose toward the front door, and Aaron was out the door in a flash. He ran over to the closest tree at the edge of the woods. He fought with his pajama pants string. Aaron stood there and sighed in relief.

All of a sudden, he realized he wasn't alone. *Tap, tap, tap.* Aaron slowly pulled up his pajamas and walked backward away from the woods. Ten feet away from him was one of the largest spiders he had ever seen. The spider was looking at Aaron, and Aaron was look-ing at the spider. Aaron kept backing up. The spider didn't move. Aaron felt as if its eyes were following him. About fifty yards from the house, he made a run for it.

When Aaron made it back to the living room and realized all the girls were sitting at the table in the dining room, chowing down.

"Late for breakfast again," Paul said. "You owe me, or you would not have any sausage."

Aaron rolled his eyes. "Story of my life," he muttered.

The group were sitting there finishing up their breakfast when Ms. Blue came into the room. She was dressed in a long, elegant olive-green traveling cloak. "I'll be back within a day—sometime midday tomorrow. Alissa, you are in charge. Have the girls work on pages thirty to forty-two in their herb and plant identification books. Include our new guests. Remember, no one is to know who you are." Everyone turned and looked at her. "The more I thought about it, the more I realized we need to deal with this sooner rather than later. Paul informed me of the men at the dock when you made your arrival. That means there will be others who know where you are. So, to avert a witch war or a war with the rest of the World Under, we need to act swiftly." Out the door she went.

Aaron quickly went to the door to see where she went. Ms. Blue clicked her fingers. Within two minutes, the large spider he had seen earlier in the morning was standing there. Ms. Blue climbed up onto its back, and away she went. Aaron returned to the table.

"When was this?" Miranda asked. She hated it when the adults didn't include them.

"Ms. Blue got up early and made some morning coffee. Mighty nice of her. Miss Alissa, may I have another cup?" Paul requested. Alissa poured more coffee into a bowl on the floor. "I think I am in heaven. I have not had coffee in a while, and this is quite good."

Miranda took a different approach. "So where is Ms. Blue headed?"

"You may as well know, because I do not necessarily want to deal with your emotionally moody self all day," Paul said. "Ms. Blue is headed to speak with the chief witch. They will most likely seek counsel with the wizard guild as well. The biggest question is what to do with or for you two. We will not know anything until she returns. We also need to find out how Emma is doing. I miss Lily already."

"But she turned you into a goat!" Aaron said with a confused look on his face.

Paul just went into the other room and lay down by the fire.

CHAPTER 19

A Direction to Be Taken

FINALLY, THREE DAYS LATER, MS. BLUE RETURNED. They were out in the courtyard, playing ball with Squeaks. Even Toad seemed to be enjoying the games. The kids, including a few extra young girls from their classes, were standing in a large circle with their toes touching each other. They stood as if they were each riding a horse. They would toss a volleyball back and forth to one another. The individual who caught the ball last in a series of six passes had to launch the ball straight up as high as possible, but the ball had to come back down inside the circle. Squeaks was flying circles around the outside of the kids' circle. She had to shoot under that person's legs, catch the ball on her nose, and return it to the player the thrower had called out, all without dropping it. Occasionally, Toad would give it a try.

Ms. Blue stood on the porch, watching the game with Paul. Apparently, the kids had not seen her return. "Paul," Ms. Blue said, and Paul nodded, but he kept watching the kids. "The chief wants you gone. She wants this problem of being involved with you gone as well. To think we are looking at the two most powerful people in the World Under. Simple kids. You must prepare them for that. It's amazing how quickly we forget what it's like to be young."

Squeaks grabbed the ball with her nose and took it to the next player. *Thunk.* She must have heard Ms. Blue's voice. She had dropped the ball.

Alissa screamed, "Last one to the cottage is a poison mushroom!"

All the kids took off running and circled around Ms. Blue. The young girls from the tribe were excused, except Alissa. Once the young witches were out of earshot, Ms. Blue engaged the group. Paul moseyed down from the porch and took a place in the back of the circle. Everyone was quiet as they waited for Ms. Blue to address them.

She looked around the circle and made eye contact with each one. "The chief wishes that we do not delay. She also wishes that we prove you twins are truly the royal children."

Miranda had an odd look on her face. Aaron spoke first. "How do we do that?" he asked.

Ms. Blue continued. "Apparently, your escort and protector here notified a wizard from his guild that both the royal babies had survived the siege. Then a wizard hurried off and sealed off portions of the palace years ago when your parents were killed. At that time Paul had set in place a plan that would prove your legitimacy to the senate, a risky plan, but one that may work with the help of the witches. Only those with royal blood would be able to venture into those sealed spaces. We are going to use some ancient magic of the order: circles within circles of a circle. This will take place at eight o'clock tomorrow morning. Everyone will meet in this field. There are wizards from the guilds who are going to help. You will be tested. If you pass the first test, we will move quickly to the Senate of the World Under. From there, we will go and test you both. With that proof, we will reengage the Senate so that they are aware of your rightful standing. There will be a little trickery involved, but I think if everything goes as planned, by the end of the day, you will be very much safer in this world. So, I suggest we all have a relaxing dinner. Tomorrow is going to be an eventful and interesting day."

CHAPTER 20

The Magical Circles

THE GROUP GOT UP EARLY THE NEXT DAY. THAT MORN-ing, Paul had them pack their backpacks again, possibly for another move, not knowing where that move would be to.

Abigail leaned over to Squeaks. "Did you hear any of the adults talking last night?"

Squeaks said, "No."

"Drat," Miranda said.

"They must have magic for that," Aaron said.

Paul sidled up to them and winked, and Miranda looked annoyed. "Do you have your bags ready?" Paul asked. Everyone said yes. Even Alissa had a bag this time. Ms. Blue had said to pack it just in case. Paul turned to Aaron. "Do you have the ball?" he asked.

"Yeah, but why?" Aaron responded.

"Just curious," Paul said. "We might find a time when we have to whittle away the hours of the day. Besides, I find your games quite entertaining."

The group moved out of Ms. Blue's living room onto the porch. "The first place we will go today will be the Senate," Ms. Blue said.

Everyone could hear a rustle off in the distance. Apparently, Tribe Four would be joining them. As the coven of witches marched closer, they noticed the witches were wearing different robes and different hats. The robes were dark brown. The hats matched. The hats had black rings around them, and the tops were scrunched down. They had magic wands like those of Tribe Two. Another dozen witches from Tribe Two then emerged from the side of the cottage. Tribe Two all wore dark green. Tribe Four had formed a large circle out in the middle of the field. They left an opening for the group to enter through. Tribe two marched down through the opening and formed their own second circle inside of the first circle.

There was a flash of light, and out of nowhere six ancient wizards were standing in the center of the circle, as well as a witch in a red robe from one of the other three witch tribes. The witches from Tribe Two motioned for everyone to join the circle. As everyone was entering the circle, a short wizard approached. He was a couple inches shorter than the twins. The wizard was sporting a navy-blue jacket with white top hat and white trousers. He carried a knotty walking stick. His beard and mustache were of medium length, and he wore piercings in his nose and ear. As he approached, he stuck his stick in the ground and pulled on a pair of white gloves. Stopping in front of Miranda, he pulled out a purple velvet bag and a small stone knife that looked more like a long arrowhead. Then he reached out and cut off a chunk of Miranda's bangs. Dropping the hair into the purple bag, he turned toward Aaron. Taking two more steps, he grabbed Aaron by the hair, and then, with the stone knife, he cut Aaron's face on his left cheek.

"Ouch." Aaron flinched and turned away.

Miranda jumped forward and pushed the wizard back two steps. "What's wrong with you?" she demanded.

"I'm sorry," replied the wizard. "I should have told you I was going to do that, I think." After dropping the bloody knife into the bag, taking a couple puffs of his pipe. He blew the smoke into the bag, the wizard shouted, "Crowns to be seen in smoke, hair, and blood! To share with all, do these share a royal family line?" Opening the bag, he watched the smoke rise out. He immediately dropped to one knee, bowing toward the twins.

The smoke rose high above the crowd. It had morphed into two interlaced identical red smoke crowns. The rest of the wizards bowed, as did Paul. He dropped onto his front knees, pressing his horns onto the ground.

The small wizard stood. "The Dunkeld family has survived! They have passed the wizards' test. They are the true heirs to the throne. Long live the princess and the prince!" He quickly went back to stand with his fellow wizards in their circle.

Then a tall witch from Tribe Four directed everyone. The six wizards took up spaces forming their own circle within the other two circles. The rest of Tribe Two helped to fill in the circles empty spaces closing all the circles. That left Paul, Miranda, Aaron, Alissa, Abigail, and Ms. Blue standing in the center of all three circles. Aaron got a good look at the short, squat witch in red, and he shook his head. Miranda looked at the two closest wizards. One was wearing a smooth metallic-looking robe and matching hat. Around the brim were all sorts of different-colored mushrooms that looked as if they were growing out of his head. He had exceptionally long, curly black hair and a short, well-trimmed beard and mustache. The other wizard wore a brown robe that had little green leaves growing out of it everywhere. His hat was similar. Smelling of mint, he turned around, and Miranda got a good look at his face. Half his face was a normal old man's face, and the other half was covered in yellowish-green scales, as was one of his hands. He held a small green snake that kept moving around.

The short, squat witch announced with a deep, booming voice that they would move to the Senate in two minutes. That brought everyone's attention back to her. She was wearing deep red robes trimmed in gold and black. She had a large black wart on her nose.

"Everyone must focus on the image of the stone floor at the bottom of the Senate stairs."

Ms. Blue pulled a gold watch out of the pocket in her traveling cloak and then put it back in. "It is time!" she yelled.

The tall wizard with the yellowish-green scales pulled a magic wand out of his sleeve where the snake was. He pointed the wand straight up in the air, toward the root system above. He started moving his magic wand in large, slow circles. The root started to flash with lights, as if electricity were running back and forth through the ceiling of the cavern. He hollered out in a scratchy hissing voice, "*Tilg mac lorg seanadh!*"

There were crackling sounds. They felt pressure in their eardrums, and— *poof!* —the group were standing on a large stone walkway at the bottom of a large set of stairs heading up to a grand-looking building.

Miranda spoke in awe. "We've been transported through thin air." As she looked around, all the witches and wizards in the circle raised their heads.

"Okay, remember, timing is very important," Ms. Blue said. "The Senate should have just begun." She waved a hand in the air. "I need a runner. Miss Cindy, if you would do the honor."

A young girl in the second circle from Tribe Two came forward.

"Announce to the Senate that the tribes of witches would like to be invited to address the Senate," Ms. Blue said.

"Yes, ma'am," Cindy called out as she proceeded to run up the stairs.

The old wizard with the mushrooms on his hat said, "We might as well start climbing the steps."

Paul told the group, "For the most part, timing is everything today. You see, we want to catch the Senate off guard. After they start their session, which they already have, and before they really get going into doing any regular business. At the beginning of the day, they always address new business."

Everyone could hear the young girl hollering as she ran through the doors at the top of the stairs. "The tribes request an invitation!"

Cindy was back within a few minutes. She was sweating and breathing hard. The invitation had been granted. The group was already halfway up the stairs. The building was massive. It was a powerful sight. They felt humbled just to stand before it. It had fifty pillars surrounding the perimeter, supporting the roof overhangs, similar to those of the ancient Roman Colosseum. The overhang was graced with chiseled figures, including some riding spider-pulled chariots, brandishing whips and spears. There were huge cyclops figures, giants surrounded by small dragons, and large crocodiles marching back toward the chariots—the scene of a massive battle. As they got closer to the building, they noticed statues of gargoyles and lions in front of the great pillars. Behind the pillars were a large walkway, a courtyard, and two silver doors, which opened as if by magic. The group passed through the great doors.

The parlor within was just as impressive, with large pictures of witches, wizards, and all sorts of World Under creatures. There were also statues of animals known on the surface, such as dinosaurs and reptiles of all different types. It was like walking through a weird, magical museum. On the opposite side of the room was another set of massive silver doors, which opened automatically as well. As they opened, they could hear the commotion of the people inside. They passed through the doors and were standing at the top of what seemed like bleacher-type seating in a large amphitheater. It was a semicircle of stairs and seats as well as tables filled with scrolls and papers, the people sat behind the cluttered tables. The group slowly worked their way to the ground floor.

A young man down below hollered, "The tribes of witches are given permission to address the International World Under Senate!"

The squat witch with the wart on her nose spoke first. "It is I, Chief Wart Berry of the Fifth Tribe of Witches," she said.

"And I, Ambassador Blue of the Second Tribe of Witches," Ms. Blue called out.

The tall witch from tribe four spoke next. "And I, Chief Star Fire of the Fourth Tribe of Witches.

The short wizard spoke next. "And I Master Sandor Connor Steven McDowell active Chief Grandmaster of the Wizarding Guild of Glasgow."

Then Paul addressed the crowd. "I, Sir Paul Andrew Scott McTrustry of the Third Wizarding Guild of Glenmore, in the wizards' hole and acting captain of the royal guard."

The twins looked at Paul.

Ambassador Blue stepped forward. "Our business is that we have granted asylum to members of the royal family and wish to let it be known."

The room erupted into chaos, with people pointing, shouting, and running with papers. Aaron looked around at all the commotion. Miranda was taking in the magnificent buildings design and was amazed.

There were beautiful purple draperies hanging all around the walls, as well as pictures of famous figures, none known to her. Most of them looked to be of royal standing, most likely from the past, possibly the twins' late relatives. This world was foreign to her but one she could belong to. The chamber had chandeliers hanging everywhere, with candles burning like thousands of sparkly lights. In the bottom center stood a podium on a dais with a line of five massive chairs. The center chair sat higher than the rest behind the speaker's pulpit. Behind the chairs were three large arched windows with an amazing view of the root system above London's cavern. On each side of the massive windows were grand double doors, likely leading to the private chambers of the Senate judges. Above the entire room was an amazing arched dome surrounded by hand-carved stone gargoyles on the edge of a balcony.

At the mention of the witches' business, a tall man dressed in a deep purple robe with a gold cape and a purple-and-gold crown stood up from the center chair and walked to the podium. A man in a suit just below the dais announced, "Grand Chancellor Neiman approaches the podium!"

Grand Chancellor Neiman raised his hand, "That's a pretty hefty claim to make to start off a normal day. That it is. And what proof is there of this claim?"

The wizard with the blue jacket addressed the chancellor. "We wish the Senate to put them to a test."

The twins looked at each other.

The chancellor replied, "What kind of test even exists to see if one is royalty?"

The wizard replied, "The test exists by the fact that you stand here in this meager form of grandeur instead of sitting on the throne itself in the center of the entire World Under. I see you are powerless to enter there, or that's where we would all be standing. You are powerless to enter the royal king and queen's palace chambers, which I sealed myself with the kings very blood the night their lives were taken from the World Under."

They could see a faint but growing look of disdain on the chancellor's face. Somebody spoke from the back of the Senate Hall: "There is a test! Let's see them tested! The test is simple. Only those with the DNA of the royal line will be able to enter those chambers."

The chancellor stood there for a long moment. Another witch stood up to his right from one of the other four chairs. Three other judges' chairs were empty. She walked forward and whispered in his ear.

"Very well," the chancellor said. "We shall test these two."

Chief Wart Berry spoke next. Some of the witches and wizards formed a new circle. The rest backed halfway up the steps, forming a second circle around the chamber.

Chief Wart Berry said, "Chancellor, if you would be so kind as to pick out three of your fellow colleagues, then we shall pop off to the palace and be right back in no time, knowing whether or not these youngsters are of the royal line."

The Senate judge in purple and gold came down and stood by the chancellor. He pointed to two other senators close to the front, who stepped forward and walked behind her.

"Very well. Let's get this grand show over with," Chancellor Neiman said.

Ms. Blue raised her hand. Eight witches and two wizards came down the steps and formed a third inner circle around the whole party itself, Senators, Chancellor, and Group. Then just like that, they vanished from the room.

CHAPTER 21

The Royal Statement

T HE GROUP, INCLUDING THE GRAND CHANCELLOR and his chosen senators, found themselves standing on a marble walkway featuring a beautiful herringbone pattern of whites and blacks. Before them stood two dozen steps, each about eight feet long, of the most beautiful greenish marble. The walkway was lined with trees and bushes. There were half a dozen stone statues of kings and queens off to each side of the steps, as well as some beautiful burial crypts surrounded by stunning flower beds. There were hedges that were pruned to look like elephants and rhinoceros lining both sides of the white marble castle walls. The walls themselves had little windows and walkways lining the tops. They were connected in the corners with eight large towers that reached up as if to meet the roots above. Four of the towers came to points with their red stone roofs. The other towers did not look to have roofs. The walkway they stood on ended behind them at the edge of a gorgeous, scenic field of colored grasses and flowers. You could see a lake off to the left of the Palace walls. A stream of water fell from the cavern ceiling into the Palace itself.

The Grand Chancellor spoke. "Let's get this over with. I have things to do." He seemed delighted to be there, entering the palace. He started up the walkway at a brisk pace.

Paul motioned for Abigail to climb onto his back. Some of the order of witches struggled to keep up. The whole group worked to keep up with the chancellor. As Chancellor Neiman approached a pair of large golden doors, he waved his right hand, and the doors opened automatically. As the group passed through, the twins were impressed. Beyond the walls was a beautiful stone palace on the other side of the courtyard's grounds. The courtyard itself was unbelievably beautiful. There were flower beds everywhere. Standing inside the outer wall you were able to see where the falling waters landed. The water from the falls was pouring out into the center of a lake in the middle of the grounds. The lake, which was shaped like a crescent moon, had two streams that ran out of opposite ends and under the palace's outer walls. There were more flower beds, and there were fountains and more sculpted hedges. A beautiful hand-chiseled white marble bridge crossed the closest stream. The railings on the bridge had dozens of different birds chiseled into the top railing.

The group moved quickly to keep up with the chancellor, who crossed the bridge and went around the tip of the lake and headed for the inner palaces arched openings. It was a Palace inside a Palace. As they made their way around the backside of the crescent moon shaped lake. They found themselves facing the most breathtaking structure. It was three stories in height. The inner Palace didn't have a roof either. The front was composed of three arches with golden doors trimmed in red that were open to the view of the moon shaped lake. To each side of the doors were the most beautiful stained-glass windows. The windows were on all the levels and sides. On the inside of the windows were dozens of rows of bookshelves, a massive library. The group made their way through the golden doors. They found, as they passed into the inner palace, they were standing in the center of the throne room. There were many doors leading off the throne room into the rest of the royal family's personal dwellings. Two catwalks surrounded the throne room, all clearly visible to the thrones themselves. There were two thrones, matching great royal chairs of gold with beautiful tables off to their sides, as well as one in front and a small table between the royal chairs. Everything had been chiseled and crafted by hand. There were red pillows lying everywhere. The tables all around seemed to be filled with items of importance to the royal couple: jewels, gems, and musical instruments.

The Grand Chancellor stopped short of the thrones to the king and queen. He pushed his hand forward as if to feel an invisible barrier. It was as if he had already been there a dozen times. The group stopped short of the chancellor and the senators standing front and center.

The wizard who had cast the magic spell to seal off the palace then spoke. "If these are the true future king or queen, let us all see." He then motioned for the twins to approach their parents' royal thrones.

Miranda looked at Aaron. They both walked forward past the chancellor, toward the thrones. The chancellor reached out, finding the force field still intact.

Abigail whispered in Paul's ear, "That is the judge who banished me—the witch in purple." Abigail seemed afraid.

Paul whispered back, "You have nothing to worry about with me by your side. Remember, you hold me wand. You are surrounded by the most powerful witches and wizards in the World Under."

The judge reached out, touched the barrier, and then said, "All this proves that they are the prince and princess, but that proof will never reach the outside of this palace."

Ms. Blue pulled the little gold watch out of her pocket again. "Don't be too sure," she said. As she looked at her watch, she called out to the prince and princess, "The wizards and witches request an invitation."

Miranda caught on, "They are certainly welcome and invited here."

The chancellor looked at the judge.

Ms. Blue counted. "Five. Four. Three. Two. One!"

Out of nowhere, the whole inner throne room was filled with senators and court officials who had been standing in the outer two circles of witches and wizards who had remained behind at the Senate.

There were people pointing and yelling: "They are the prince and princess! The Dunkelds have survived! What is to be done about this? What does this mean?"

The chancellor looked livid. The judge in purple pointed her magic wand at the group. At the same time, the group pointed their magic wands back toward the chancellor and the senate judge.

Paul spoke up. "Now, now, now, as captain of the royal guard, I warn everyone here to calm down. Nothing has changed, except now the World Under knows that the prince and princess are still live. Proof with me own eyes. I think there has been enough excitement for one day. This old goat cannot take much more."

"I think we should all return to the Senate," said Chief Wart Berry.

Aaron picked up a small scepter from the armrest of his father's throne and carefully set it down on the little table.

Miranda hopped up onto her mother's throne. "Look at all the items on the table! Aaron, this is unbelievable! She slid a couple rings onto her hand and was admiring them. You know, when Paul told us about this, I didn't believe it. Now I stand here and look at it in amazement."

"You know, Sis, I'd trade all this to have our parents with us. And Grandma and Grandpa back with us happy and well," Aaron said.

Miranda looked at him then at the scepter. "You always were quite level-headed."

"You don't have to say the words, but I know you mean that I'm the smart one," said Aaron. "I say let's go back to the tribes and find out about Grandma and Grandpa."

"Well said, Brother," Miranda replied.

Paul directed, "I say we all go back to the Senate and decide what is to be done." He turned to Aaron and Miranda. "I want you both to stay here where it is safe, until I come back here this evening. This is most likely the safest place for you."

Miranda smiled, hopped down from her mother's throne, picked up the little scepter Aaron had removed from their father's armrest, and then put it back. She picked up her backpack and slung it over her shoulder. "Come on, Aaron. Let's go back and find out what's going on." Without another word, the twins walked right past the chancellor toward Paul.

"I told you I want you to stay there," Paul said.

"Back to the Senate!" hollered Ms. Blue.

Within a minute, everyone was once again standing in the Senate chamber, including all the spectators and the surrounding circles. The judge in purple whispered into the chancellor's ear again. Then the chancellor and the judge walked back up to the dais floor and stood behind the podium. Aaron and Miranda walked over and stood beside Paul. Chancellor Neiman sat down in his high seat of honor.

The judge in purple and gold addressed the audience. "The twins shall be sent to one of the well-known orphanages since they have no parents, until they are of age."

Paul muttered under his breath at the twins, "You just made me life a heck of a lot more complex. I told you to stay there." Paul then addressed the Senate, "I, as active captain of the royal guard and guardian to the royal line for the past ten years, must disagree. That would not be in the royals best interest, nor would it be the safest course of action."

The judge said, "Then what would you do? Allow eleven-year-olds to rule the World Under?"

"Hardly," the chancellor mocked.

Ms. Blue cleared her throat. "The twins have been given asylum on the grounds of Tribe Two. We did not know they were of the royal family, but we gave asylum, nonetheless. A tricky old wizard fooled us all." She turned and looked at Paul. "They are too young to rule, and the witches would not stand for their involvement in the witches private matters or community. It would lead to an all-out witch war, possibly even spilling over into the rest of the caverns affairs. So, I can only see one solution. The royals are privately tutored until they are of age to rule. They can attend one of the World Unders private magical schools. As an ambassador, I offer my knowledge at this time. I will work with them until they are young adults and capable of taking on their roles in the World Under."

At that, the Senate broke out into more hollering and arguing behind them.

Paul spoke again. "Me duty does not end here! Until they are adults and can release me from me vow, I am subject to protect them. All members of the wizard guild are subject to protect them until they are at least of age."

That caused even greater chaos in the background.

A voice from the back yelled, "What of the slave girl, the tree?"

The judge in purple strode forward, raising her hands in silence, and after a long minute, everyone's eyes were on her. "What of the deciduous clan member? I, Senate High Judge Aurelie Lenoir, banished her myself! Did the guards let you back in out of pity?"

Abigail started to shake. Aaron took a half dozen steps forward. He yelled up at the judge, making a fist. There was a ripple of pressure in the air. "I FORBID IT!"

Paul whispered into Miranda ear, "Quickly—do not let him make a fool of himself. Pardon her."

Miranda rushed up to the side of her brother. Putting a hand on his shoulder, she proclaimed, "I, Miranda, your princess and future queen, pardon Miss Abigail Eberleaf and list her as one of my first personal advisers to the World Under."

The bold move was too much for the governing body to handle. The Senate went into hysterics, with more screaming and shouting. The noise was deafening.

Miranda hollered at the top of her lungs, "And furthermore we shall accept Ambassador Blue's offer!" She pulled at her brother, and they both exited quickly toward Paul.

"Let us hurry before we find out they have decided to hang us instead," Paul said.

Leaving behind most of the witches and wizards, Paul took all the kids and left quickly. They hurried up the steps, out the doors, and down the steps toward where they first had appeared. It did not take long for a dozen witches to catch up and form a circle around Paul and the kids, and they found themselves back in Ms. Blue's courtyard.

CHAPTER 22

Prince and Princess

THE GROUP THOUGHT EVERYONE ELSE WOULD BE BACK within a half hour or so. They were wrong. The rest of the witches and wizards did not return until well after midnight. Ms. Blue walked up onto the porch and sat down in a little rocking chair, looking at the kids. Paul moseyed out and spoke to his old comrades. They all seemed happy to see him. Paul came back to the porch as the wizards took one another's hands, and they were gone. All the witches of the two tribes stood in a large group, chatting like longtime friends.

As Paul made his way back to the porch, Ms. Blue addressed him. "You know there are going to be repercussions for this. Tribe One and Tribe Three disagree with our decision. There are many others in the World Under who would like to see the twins dead. Half the

Senate disapproves, but the other half adore them and are encouraged by their survival."

The kids were laughing, and Squeaks was doing her thing. She was miming eating a sandwich in front of the new company of witches. Aaron was standing beside a rock on which Abigail was sitting, ignoring Squeaks. A lot of the other young witches were rolling with laughter.

Abigail leaned toward Aaron. "Thank you," she said, and she laid her head on his shoulder. He put his arm around her.

Alissa and Miranda were some distance away. Miranda finally seemed to come to terms with her brother's affection for their new friend.

Ms. Blue said, "Tribe Two has decided to take an unfortunate approach to keep the peace with Tribe One and Tribe Three. I have been assigned permanent ambassador of education to the royal court and banished from tribal leadership. I think I'm fine with that. In fact, since we are coming up on the fall equinox, I will probably go find out what needs to be done for their schooling. I assume you will stay on the same course. A vow of protection? But before I can do that, I have to address Alissa's situation. She is old enough to emancipate herself. She can continue studies with another mentor or continue to assist me while I find out about the kids' schooling. Chief Wart Berry even offered to take her on as a personal apprentice. I will leave that up to her since she can no longer be my apprentice under Tribe Two. Oh, and by the way, as for Abigail, Miranda's pardon was not accepted by the Senate. She must remain someone's property. So, she belongs to you, Paul."

Paul shook his head, muttering, "What evil these people hold in their hearts, Ms. Blue did you feel a ripple of pressure in the air when Aaron ran forward to stop the Senate?"

"I did," Ms. Blue confessed, "and that has emboldened my feelings about staying with the twins. It will only cost me my leadership in Tribe Two. This is definitely a new road in my life that I never would have envisioned. There is a prophecy among witches. I'll fill you in later. It's quite lengthy. It's about a king who can stop time."

Paul pointed out, "The kid could hardly cause a flicker of light out of the end of me magic wand, though if he does have such an ability, the kids will be in more danger than ever." Ms. Blue added, "Chief Wart Berry also noticed it, and if she did, half a dozen others did too. It will be interesting to see what this next school year brings. We will have to be on our guard."

"Did the Senate indicate which school?" Paul questioned.

"No." Ms. Blue answered.

Paul responded, "Good. Then I may have another trick up me sleeve. Do you know how to play poker? I think we have been delt a good hand. We will have some choices. The Senate will assume we will enroll the kids in one of the large magical schools of the World Under. I know of an almost forgotten school for orphaned boys. The schools are, as we speak, gathering in Sagano, at the Bamboo Temple. They will be waiting for the Great Root to wake up and gift the newest students with magical wands."

Ms. Blue stood up and hollered for Alissa and the rest of the group. "Everyone inside. We need something to eat, and then to bed with you. Alissa, I need to speak with you in the morning. Paul, you may be one of the craftiest wizards I know. But don't let it go to your head."

Ms. Blue headed inside, and Paul followed.

The journey does not end here.
Read on
to enjoy me crazy goat and
his companions in
book two:
A Shadow Ascends.

A Shadow Ascends

Trickery of a Magical Goat

RJ WYATT

Coffee Needed

T HE NEXT DAY WAS A LONG AND EXCITING ONE. ALL of a sudden, Ms. Blue's tiny corner of the World Under seemed to explode with activity. There were dozens of kids, mostly young witches and those soon to be. There were witches who came from Tribe Four, and there were many witches from Tribe Two. The courtyard and the house were filled with activity. A lot of the witches brought their significant others with them.

"I'm surprised how many witches get married," Miranda said to Ms. Blue.

"Sure, they do, Miranda. We have our own society and our own way of doing things, but that doesn't mean we don't enjoy life like the rest of the world. Not all of these witches have the magical ability you kids have. Some of them only deal with potions and herbal remedies or cures. A lot of them have mates who have nothing to do with the tribe itself."

Ms. Blue continued, "They live in little towns around the tribal lands, but some of them live in the cities like Poland or Berlin. There are even witches and wizards here tonight who came from as far as England and the Scottish Irish caverns. They came to see and meet the future royals, knowing someday their communities may be under royal rule again. They hope for a good one."

The twins were bombarded with gifts and greetings.

A lot of young couples were showing up. They had built a bonfire. Abigail walked up with Aaron beside her.

"How long will this last, Ms. Blue?" Aaron pointed out to his sister that a group of kids were picking teams for soccer on the west side of Ms. Blue's field.

Ms. Blue told them, "Enjoy the activities. They will last long into the night or at least till folks start acting like fools and make boobs out of themselves. Hurry—go play before you miss out."

More adults set up tables and chairs; many brought their own. They brought so much food that Aaron and Squeaks would be enjoying it for days to come. The older folks seemed to start to disappear around eleven o'clock, while younger groups kept arriving. The kids all roasted apples, hot dogs, and marshmallows until the fire got too hot to get close to. Some of the young couples brought barrels of their own mead. It didn't take long for the cookout to turn into an all-out party, the kind Miranda and Aaron would probably never have seen at Grandma and Grandpa's farm. It seemed a lot of the witches and wizards and their significant others were getting, loaded, to say the least. The evenings' activities had taken a turn for the worse.

Finally, sometime a little after midnight, Ms. Blue had had enough. She called out from the porch, "Looks like everyone's welcome is over!"

There was a lot of grumbling. Abigail heard a young witch call out from the back, cackling and giggling, "Last one to the lower dance field has to drink a double flagon!"

All of a sudden, forty or fifty young adults took off running in a northern direction. "Okay, the party is over!" Ms. Blue exclaimed.

Paul headed into the house. A few couples ran out the front door, laughing. "I wonder where they were," Paul said to himself. He shook his head. "Just as I remember, and we were so young."

"Girls, upstairs, please; it's time to end this day," Ms. Blue said. "Squeaks, to the roost."

Toad had gone up there three to four hours ago. Squeaks flew up to the cupola and was asleep in minutes. Alissa, Abigail, and Miranda headed upstairs. Paul lay down by the fireplace. The fire in the fireplace had just about gone out. Ms. Blue walked over and placed some fresh logs on top of the hot embers. She then waved her wand and spoke, *"fa's."* The fire flared up from the center of the coals. She turned to Aaron and said, "Good night, young man." She started to climb the steps but stopped. She turned her head and addressed Aaron again. "Thank you, Aaron."

"For what?" Aaron replied.

There was a soft smile on Ms. Blue's face. "For caring enough for your young friend to stick your neck out," she replied.

Aaron squinted up at her. "Anybody would have done it, Ms. Blue," he said.

Paul spoke up. "No, Aaron, most people would not have done it, especially in front of the entire World Under governing body."

Ms. Blue raised a hand as if to say, *Wait till I finish.* "Young man, you could have very easily been made to be a fool. Thank you, Aaron, for being strong enough not to stand by and let Miss Abigail be mistreated. But know this: you did not need to do that. There are many adults around you who would have intervened. It would have been wiser of you not to show your views on the treatment of the evergreens for now. Good night." She turned and proceeded to climb the stairs.

"Good night, Ms. Blue," Aaron called after her.

She smiled as she went.

At that moment, in a stone house deep in the cavern of the black forest, there was a meeting underway. The grand chancellor stood staring up at a tall, dark wizard, surrounded by a dozen of his closest followers. Many of them were senators and businessmen. They all had one thing in common: they were all members of the New Croatoan Order of Druids.

Chancellor Neiman addressed the group. "It won't be long. We have taken out three senate judges this last year, and there are a dozen other senators I want to disappear. You know who they are!" he exclaimed.

Some of the druids bowed to their master as they entered the room.

"I will meet with each and every one of you to give you your assignments," the tall wizard then spoke. He addressed the chancellor and the governing body. "Chancellor, you have performed as I knew you would for our Order. You may go, and as for everyone else they may leave as well for this evening. Thank you, my brother."

The chancellor then addressed the senators. "I will meet with each one of you regarding whom you are to promote to be replacements." They all looked at one another with delight. The chancellor looked to his brother druid master for approval. He received a nod from his brother druid. The chancellor was delighted as well.

"I would have you all stay and dine with me, but I have one or two items of business to take care of myself. You are all excused, except for my favorite judge," the druid master said. "I have one more job for you, so stay, and we can take care of that together."

The judge waited until the rest of the group had left the dwelling.

"My companion and I are going to call on a few of his friends," said the druid master.

Just then, the Croatoan druid master's shadow moved. It started to slowly glide across the floor and climbed the far wall of the stone house. Slowly it left the wall like a ghost. It separated from him. The candlelight didn't seem to affect it. The judge looked up at the shadow with a look of admiration and fear. The shadow moved around the room and took up a position behind the judge. It slid into the side of her head. She went rigid. The judge's black cat with purple eyes shot out the door. After a minute or two, the shadow detached from the judge and floated over to the druid master. The two merged again.

"Send me three young apprentices from Tribe Three and be quick about it!" he said to the judge.

The judge hurried outside in an all-out run and caught up with her cat. She pulled out a small crystal stone and spoke into it. It wasn't long before three young witch apprentices arrived. They entered the stone house as the judge peeked in the window. The shadow overtook the three young ladies. They all stood there rigidly and then dropped to the floor. The only things left were the winged skeletal imprints of what was left of the girls' souls, their shadows. The three shadows floated up and began circling the druid master getting their orders. Next, they shot out the door weaving back and forth in the direction of the next cavern, Berlin (the witches tribal lands).

The next morning felt like it came early. At seven o'clock, Ms. Blue made her way down the steps. She had a look of irritation on her face. "I see a mister and a miss in close proximity, where they should not be."

Paul turned and looked at her. "They are twins. Besides, Miranda said she was dizzy and felt sick. She said she had a ringing in her head, and it was making her nauseous." Miranda was lying on the opposite end of the sofa from Aaron. "Don't be too hard on her. Besides, I said it was okay. What are the chances for some of that great coffee of yours?"

"The chances are always better if you don't defy my rules. It undermines my authority and it also sets a bad precedent." she stated grumpily.

"Okay I apologize," Paul said, "it will not happen again. Next time, I will send her back upstairs or get you meself. Is that better?"

"That will do, and I will gladly get you some coffee. I need some myself." Ms. Blue stopped and then turned and looked down at Paul. "Paul, and what of Abigail?"

Paul got up and followed Ms. Blue to the kitchen as they discussed schools. Paul said, "We will include Abigail. Like I said, I am thinking of an almost

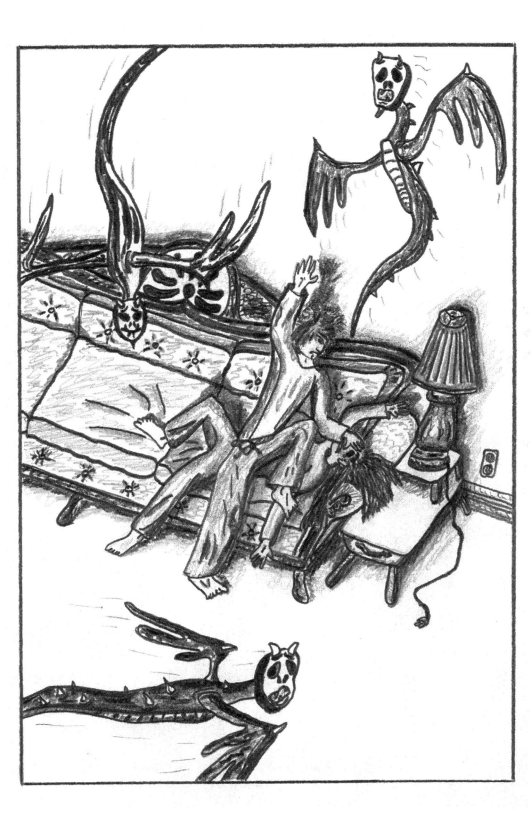

unheard-of orphan school: VanDyne's Wizarding Academy for lost boys."

Aaron rolled over. He blinked toward the light coming from the kitchen. Then he looked at his sister. What he saw threw his reflexes into a panic: there were three black shadows spinning around Miranda. They were taking turns sliding into the side of her head and exiting through her chest, as if she weren't even there. She kept tossing and squirming.

Aaron jumped up and screamed, "No!" He jumped on top of his sister. He shook her by the shoulders. "No, no, no, no!" he kept repeating. He pulled his hand back and slapped her hard. She wouldn't wake up. He slapped her again. Then again hitting her harder every time.

Ms. Blue reentered the room. Paul was right behind her. She set a lantern down on the end table, lighting up the whole area. The shadows fled from the light. Ms. Blue caught Aaron's hand just as he pulled back to slap Miranda again. Miranda's head was spinning as she opened her eyes.

"What are you doing?" demanded Paul.

Aaron's face was sheet white. He shakily replied, "The shadows were attacking her!"

By then, the rest of the girls had made it halfway down the steps. They stood there in their nightgowns, looking across the room.

"There are no shadows here," Ms. Blue pointed out.

"There were three shadows, and they were attacking Miranda!" Aaron said forcefully. "They were diving in and out of her head and chest!"

Ms. Blue pulled Aaron off his sister and set him down at the end of the sofa. She had Miranda sit up and looked her over. She moved Miranda's head all around and looked into her eyes. They had a glazed look to them. "What do you remember, Miranda?" Ms. Blue asked.

"I don't really remember anything." Her cheek and eye were turning black and blue and swelling. Just then, she threw up all over Ms. Blue's feet. She kept retching until there was nothing left.

Aaron was standing beside Ms. Blue now. He was scared.

"Master Aaron, you say you saw shadows?" she asked him. "Are you sure? Could you guys have sneaked some mead from the party?"

Alissa replied from behind, "No ma'am, we didn't have any." Abigail shook her head also.

Just then, Squeaks and Toad joined Ms. Blue on the living room floor. Ms. Blue looked at Toad. *Croak.* Toad nodded and croaked out, "Shadows. Before you brought the light in. *Croak.* After the young boy screamed."

Ms. Blue picked up Miranda and hurried to the front door. "Mr. McTrustry, I'm taking her to the sisters. We're going to put some spells of protection around her for now. Have the girls clean the mess, including the one in the front yard." She whistled, and she and Miranda were off to see the sisters, riding the spider.

Aaron cried out, "I need to go with her!" but it was too late.

MAPS

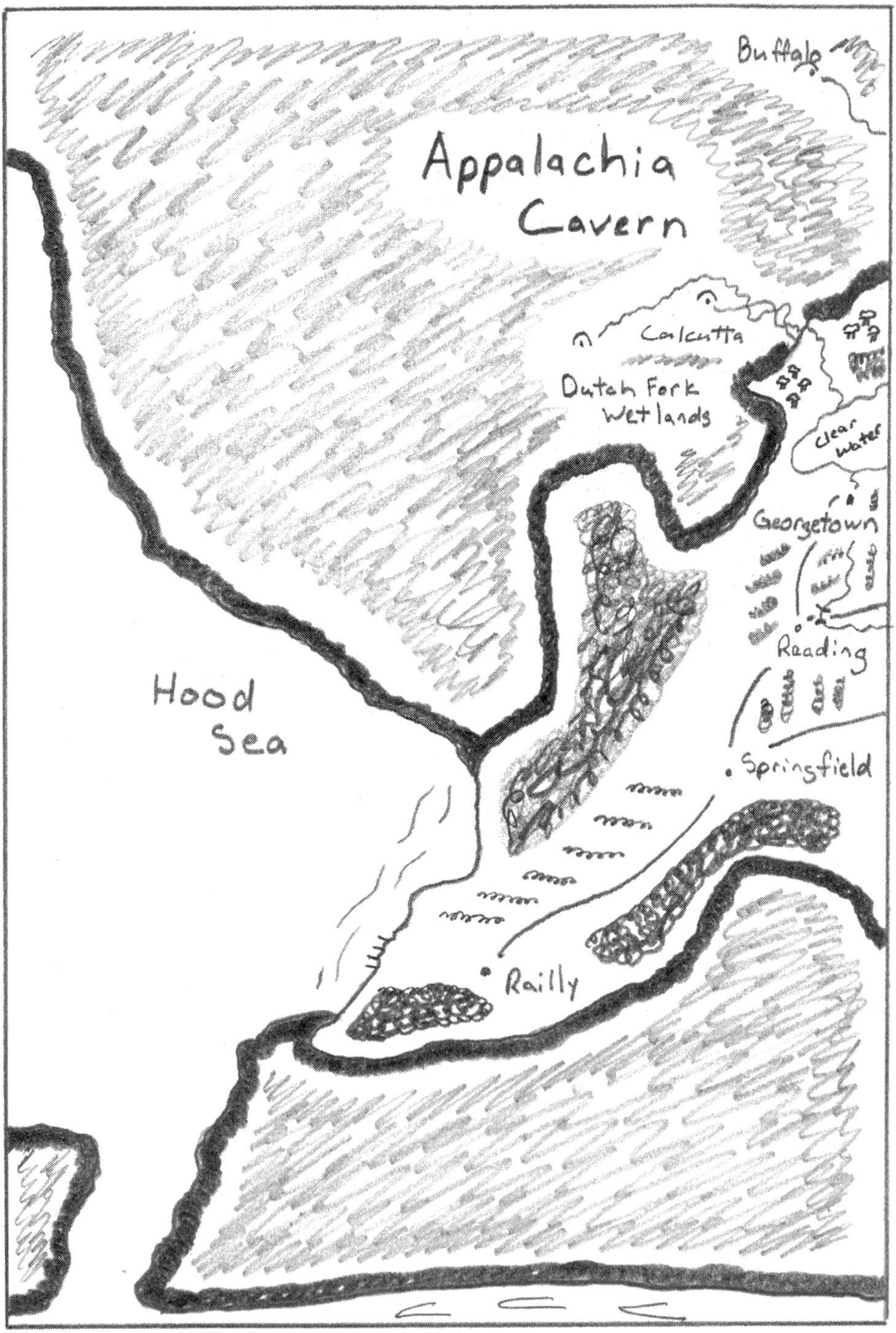
Buffalo
Appalachia
Cavern
Calcutta
Dutch Fork
Wetlands
Clear
Water
Georgetown
Reading
Hood
Sea
Springfield
Railly

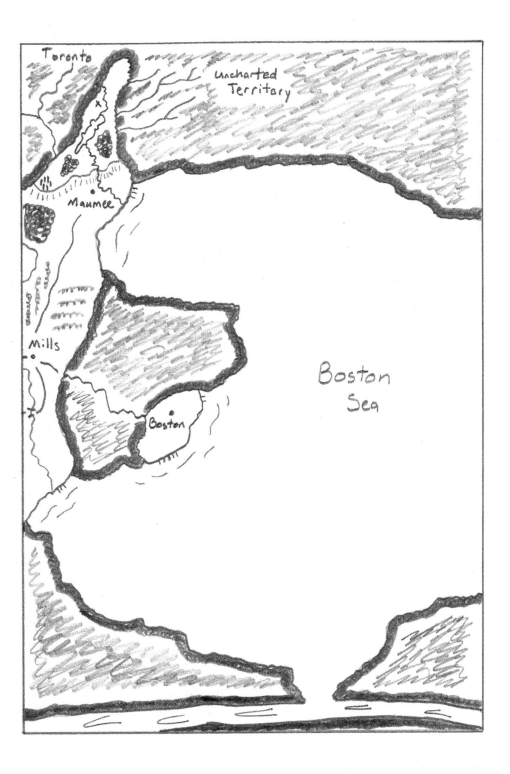

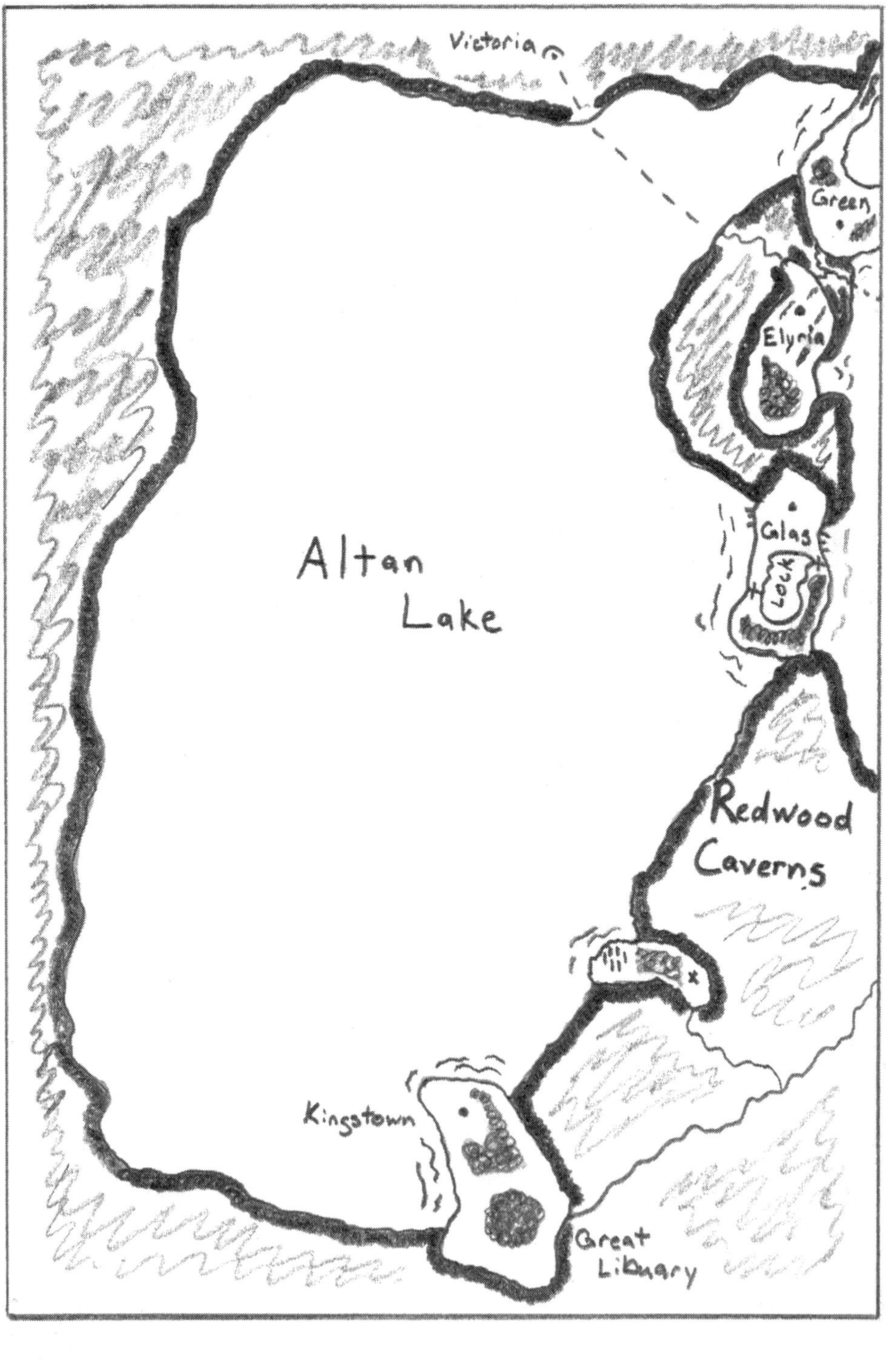
Victoria
Green
Elyria
Glas
Lock
Altan
Lake
Redwood
Caverns
Kingstown
Great
Library

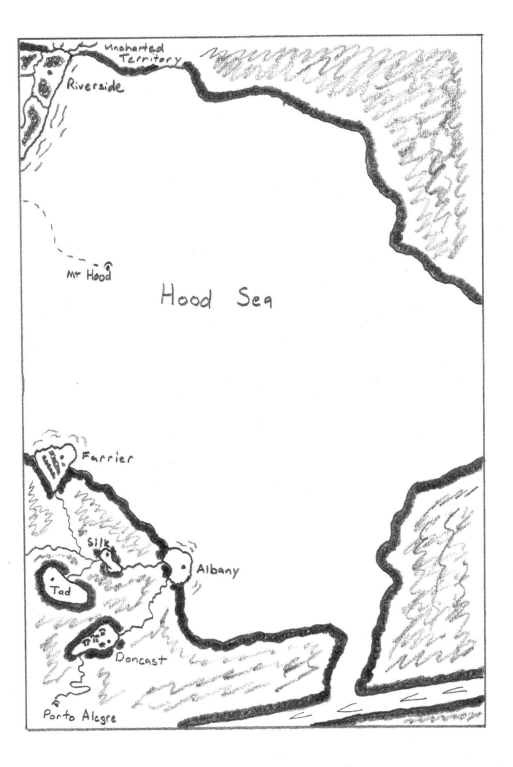

Temuco

Wood haven

Coda

Lake
Tamka

Edge of Darkness

Lighthouse

(Bay of Lights)
Réalta

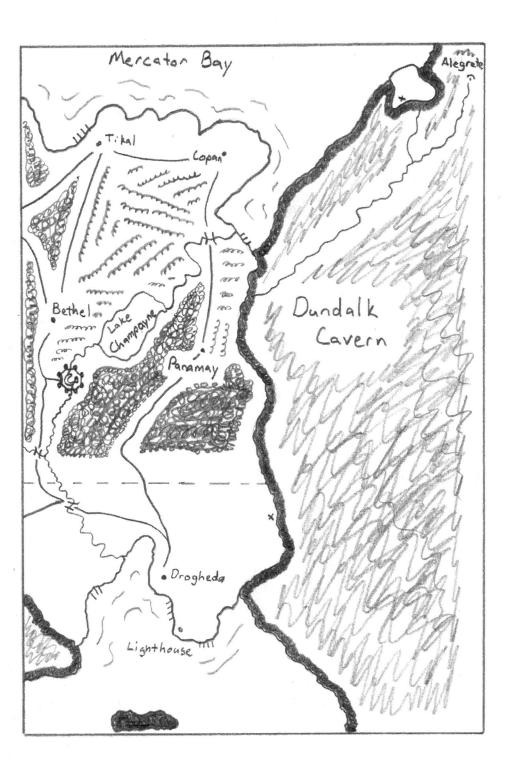

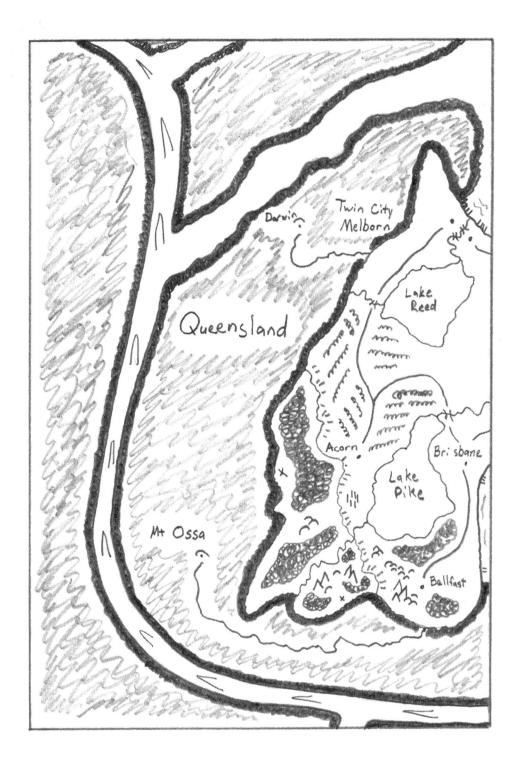

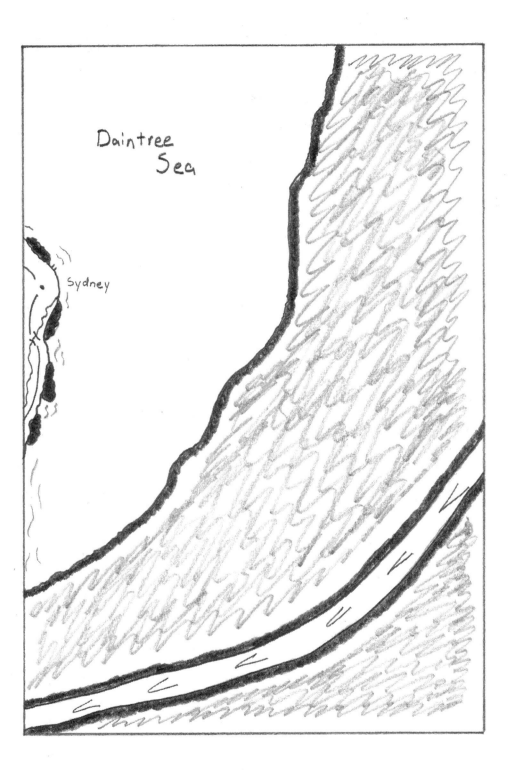

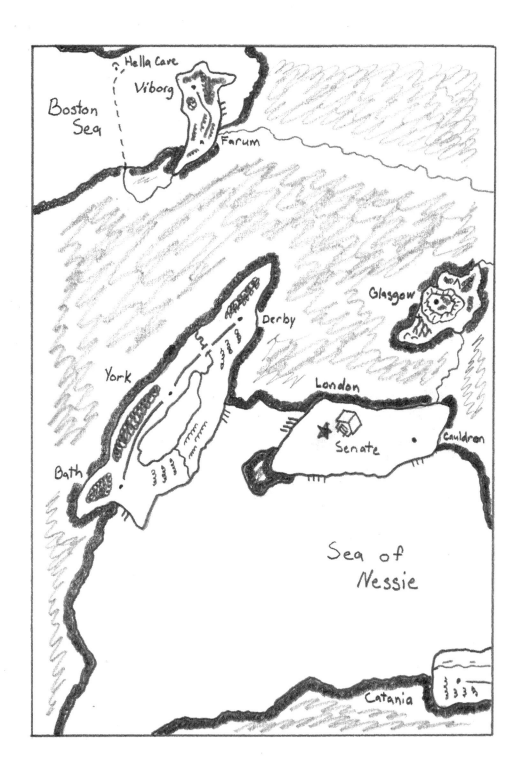

Scottish
Irish Caverns

Dunmore Caves

Uncharted Territories

Limerick

Territories Uncharted

Wartburg Castle

Poland

T4

T2

T1

T5

Munich

Dresden

Lablin

Berlin

Breman

T3

Salem

Naples

Pisa

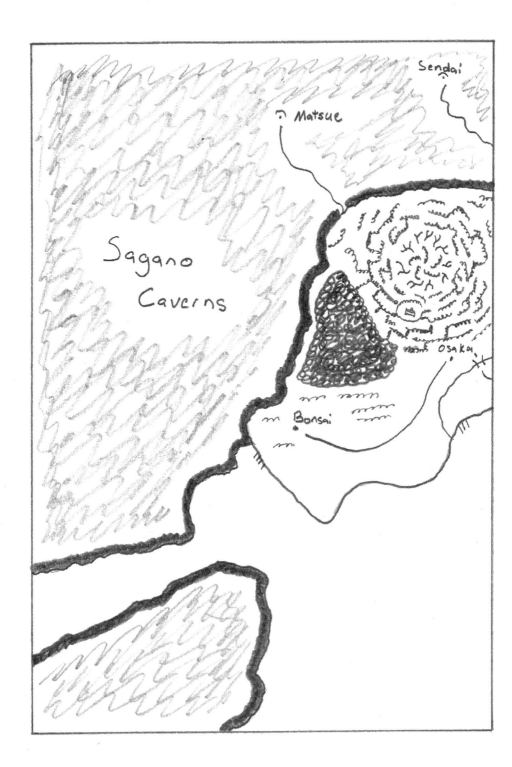

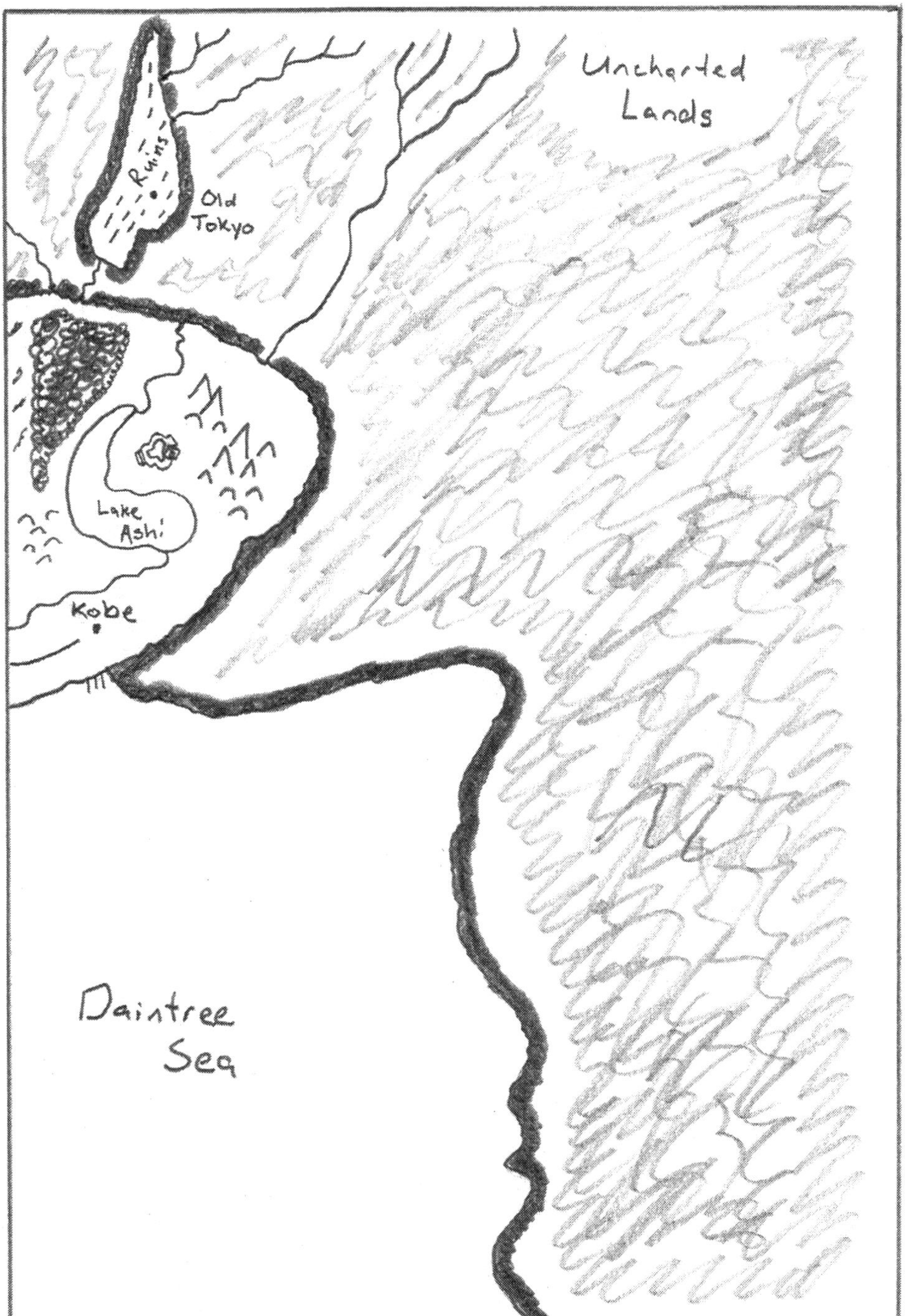
Uncharted
Lands
Ruins
Old
Tokyo
Lake
Ashi
Kobe
Daintree
Sea

GLOSSARY OF MAGICAL WORDS
(IRISH AND SCOTTISH OF OLD)

The *fada*

fada means : *long*

examples:

a	bat	a'	awful
e	bet	e'	play
i	bit	i'	feet
o	bot	o'	low
u	but	u'	flew

Lenition and eclipsis

In Lenition, an h is added after the first letter of words starting with consonants listed below. This changes the pronunciation of the letter; these variations in pronunciation are explained in parentheses.

b – bh (*v* or *w*)   c – ch (*ch* as in lo*ch*)   d – dh (*y*)

f – fh (silent)   g – gh (*ch*as in lo*ch*)   m – mh (*w*)

p – ph (*f*)   s – sh (*h*)   t – th (*h-yah*)

Eclipsis involves adding a letter before the first letter of words starting with the consonants listed below. The pronunciation of these changes are much easier, as the ellipsis is simply pronounced instead of the original first letter. In other words, the original first letter becomes silent in the case of eclipsis.

b – <u>m</u>b   c – <u>g</u>c   d – <u>n</u>d   f – <u>bh</u>f (silent)

g – <u>n</u>g   p – <u>b</u>p   t – <u>d</u>t

Glossary

abandon: *v* tre'ig

acid: *n* aige'ad

acquire: *v* faigh

age: *v* aosaigh

amethyst: *n* aimitis

amplify: *v* aimpligh

arrow: *n* saighead

barrel: *n* baraille

bend: *v* lu'b

blacken: *v* dubhaigh

block: *v* stop

blood: *n* fuil, cro'

boat: *n* ba'd

bone: *n* can'mh

bow: *v* sle'acht

bow crom: *v* before royalty (Scottish)

bracelet: *n* bra'isle'ad

break: *v* bris

breathe: *v* analaich

brilliant: *adj* lonrach

build: *v* to'gcapture: gabh

cast: *v* caith, teilg (a throw)

castle: *n* caisle'ad

clover: *n* seamair

corpse: *n* corpa'n

council: *n* comhairle

court: *n* cu'irt

cup: *n* corn, cupa'n

curse: *v* mallacht

cut: *v* ciorraigh, gearr

dance: *v* damhsa

dark: *adj* ciar

darken: *v* dall

darkness: *n* dorchacht

daylight: *n* solas

dead: *n* marbh

door: *n* doras
druid: *n* draoi
dungeon: *n* doinsiu'n
electric: *n* leictreoir
emerald: *n* sma'rag (Scottish)
end: *n* ceann, fairceann
english: *n* be'arla (langage)
enlarge: *v* me'adaich
eternal: *adj* si'orai'
eyesight: *n* radharcnasu'l
fairy: *n* sio'g
feather: *n* cleite
field: *n* faiche, gort
fire: *n* tine
fireball: *n* caor thine
fist: *n* dorn
flying: *v* eitilt
footprint: *n* lorg caise
force: *n* fo'rsa, *v* cuiriallachar
freeze: *v* reoigh, *n* sioc
goat: *n* gobhar
gold: *n* o'r
grow: *v* fa's
handwriting: *n* la'mhsri'bhneireacht
hard: *adj* crua
harden: *v* cruaigh

heal: *v* cneasaigh
hear: *v* airigh
heat: *v* te'igh
heart: *n* croi'
heartbeat: *n* buille-cridhe (Scottish)
hiccups: *n* fail
hide: *v* seithe
idiot: *adj* omadhaun, fool (Scottish)
immortal: *adj* neamhbha'smhar
invisible: *n* dofheicthe
lightning: *n* tintreach
liquid: *n* leacht, *adj* leachtach
magic: *n* asarlai'ocht, drai'ocht
magnet: *n* maighne'ad
mansion: *n* teachmo'r
map: *n* le'arsca'il
master: *n* ma'istir
mushroom: *n* fa'saonoi'che, muisriu'n
necklace: *n* muince
oath: *n* mionn
open: *v* oscail
pain: *n* pian
palace: *n* pa'la's
plant: *n* lus, *v* cuir

point: *v* di'righ
poison: *n* nimh, *v* nimhigh
prophesy: *v* tairngir, *n* tairngreacht
pull: *v* tarraing
punch: *v* dorn
push: *v* bru'
rainbow: *n* tuar ceatha
replica: *n* mac-gamhail (Scottish)
ring: *n* fa'inne
rise: *v* e'irich, (rise again, aise'irigh)
root: *n* fre'amh
rot: *v* grod (Scottish)
rot: *v* logn (Irish)
royal: *adj* ri'oga
royalty: *n* ri'ochas
ruby: *n* ru'ibi'n
sapphire: *n* saifir
scroll: *n* scrolla
secret: *n* ru'n
see: *v* feic
seer: *n* fiosaiche (Scottish)
seek: *v* cuardaigh
seize: *v* forghabh (Irish), greimich (Scottish)
senate: *n* seanad
senator: *n* seanado'ir
separate: *v* deighil

shadow: *n* sca'th
sleep: *n* codladh
slow: *v* mall
smash: *v* smiot
stone: *n* cloch
sorcerer: *n* asarlai
sorcery: *adj* asarlaiocht
straighten: *v* di'righ
strengthen: *v* la'idrigh
throw: *v* caith, teilg (Irish)
throw: *v* tilgeadh (Scottish)
trap: *n* sa'innigh
translate: *v* tiontaigh
transparent: *adj* tre'dheareacht
transport: *v* giu'lain (Scottish)
transport: *v* iompair
trap: *n* sa's
trapdoor: *v* comhla tho'ga'la
vault: *n* tuama
veil: *n* caille
village: *n* sra'idbhaile
vision: *n* aisling
void: *n* folu's
wall: *n* mu'r
wedding: *n* fainne-po'saidh (Scottish)

witch: *n* bean feasa
wizard: *n* draoi
vault: *n* tuama

THANK YOU, RECOGNITIONS AND ACKNOWLEDGEMENTS

T O ALL THAT HAVE SUPPORTED AND GUIDED ME IN this endeavor, to write the first book in this series, I thank you with Love.

1st : my better half, Lynnie, the most sexy loving beautiful person I have ever known, Thank you for being the first to see the potential in my writing of this book. As well as all the pushing involved. Recognizing the importance of these books, letting me be at small moments be that innocent 10-year-old again. Me true Flower (Lily). May we have forever together. Love XOXO

2nd : our friend Georgia, who has tolerated and worked tirelessly at this project, a solid sounding board and an example in being happy and strong at your choices in life. May you be happy in Brisbane: Ollie's cousin Georgia started out as Olivia then, was changed to honor Georgia ……. Cheers!

3rd : my family, those people chosen for you to make you the person that you are. My father and his love for his art, my mother and her love to listen to your problems a big heart, my mother-in-law who enjoys being happy and fun, to my father-in-law dearly missed a man I spent so much time with. My brothers and their interest. My wife Lynn and her siblings all the family activities and holidays I look forward to and enjoy today. Most of all my children who I love and cherish. Miranda, Douglas, Richard

4th : to all the people I work with and care for, from the very top down. CEOs I have friended to those that turn wrenches and build and design things of amazement. A team: an extended family where you are no number. A company where what goes on in your lives all matters.

5th : to small businesses that care for their customers, like the Sabatini family, helping me be a little lighter and faster today.

6th : to All American Comics, those that love books, games and simply want to stay kids.

7th : to unspoken friends, my list is too long to name, Thank You, Love RJ Wyatt

8th : to those young people that love books, me first reader Miss. M. L. G. I look forward to all the young people and their input, May they always need all of you in the Tribal Lands.

9th : to all unspoken brothers and sisters, may you go faster and farther with a clear purpose to cure and heal. Start with the hearts.

God Bless: RJ Wyatt

ABOUT THE BOOK

THIS IS A STORY ABOUT THE LIFE OF ROYAL TWINS Miranda and Aaron as they are found and recognized for their role in a magical world they were born into, the World Under. When the twins were babies, there was an attempt to eliminate the royal line from the World Under. The attempt was thought to have been a success but was not. Eventually, word of the babies' survival made it to those who wanted total control. At age ten, the twins are returned to the world they were born into. They make new friends and relations on their journey. They are guided and helped by a wizard, Paul, who is trying to live with a curse wrongly placed upon him. Paul takes the twins on a journey to a safe place, the tribal lands of the witches, while learning to overcome his handicap in his magical abilities. He also teaches the twins how to help and work with others in the process. When young Abigail Eberleaf, a girl who is half-tree and half-human, crosses Aaron's path, both of their lives change. Abigail is trying to locate and free her parents, who have been enslaved in the forced work camps of the World Under. It will take this journey across the world for her to learn how to trust again after the brutal stealing of her innocence, her childhood, and almost her life. Aaron, Miranda, and Abigail, as well as Abigail's good friend Squeaks the bat, will be joined forever as friends who grow into family with many others.

Made in the USA
Columbia, SC
30 June 2024

8367722d-738b-402d-80bb-66d37c870bd8R02